Wanted Men

A Western Duo

WALT COBURN

Thorndike Press • Waterville, Maine

"Broken Wings" first appeared in *Air Stories* (1/28). Copyright © 1927 by Fiction House, Inc. Copyright © renewed 1955 by Walt Coburn. Copyright © 2004 by Golden West Literary Agency for restored material. "Wanted Men" first appeared in Street & Smith's *Western Story Magazine* (5/30/31). Copyright © 1931 by Street & Smith Publications, Inc. Copyright © renewed 1959 by Walt Coburn. Acknowledgment is made to Condé Nast Publications for their co-operation. Copyright © 2004 by Golden West Literary Agency for restored material.

Published in 2005 by arrangement with
Golden West Literary Agency.

Thorndike Press® Large Print Western.

The tree indicium is a trademark of Thorndike Press.

The text of this Large Print edition is unabridged.
Other aspects of the book may vary from the original edition.

Set in 16 pt. Plantin by Carleen Stearns.

Printed in the United States on permanent paper.

Library of Congress Cataloging-in-Publication Data

Coburn, Walt, 1889–1971.
    [Broken wings]
    Wanted men : a western duo / by Walt Coburn.
      p. cm. — (Thorndike Press large print western)
    ISBN 0-7862-8143-X (lg. print : hc : alk. paper)
    1. Western stories.   2. Large type books.   I. Title.
  II. Thorndike Press large print Western series.
PS3505.O153B76 2005
813´.52—dc22   2005022856

Wanted Men

As the Founder/CEO of NAVH, the only national health agency solely devoted to those who, although not totally blind, have an eye disease which could lead to serious visual impairment, I am pleased to recognize Thorndike Press* as one of the leading publishers in the large print field.

Founded in 1954 in San Francisco to prepare large print textbooks for partially seeing children, NAVH became the pioneer and standard setting agency in the preparation of large type.

Today, those publishers who meet our standards carry the prestigious "Seal of Approval" indicating high quality large print. We are delighted that Thorndike Press is one of the publishers whose titles meet these standards. We are also pleased to recognize the significant contribution Thorndike Press is making in this important and growing field.

Lorraine H. Marchi, L.H.D.
Founder/CEO
NAVH

* Thorndike Press encompasses the following imprints: Thorndike, Wheeler, Walker and Large Print Press.

Table of Contents

Broken Wings

I

Two men stood near the edge of the high cliff, a stone's throw from the San Quentin lighthouse, and trained binoculars upon the fishing boat that was dropping anchor in the blue bay below. Silently, intently they watched. They exchanged glances as a skiff put out from the boat and came crawling toward the shoreline. Again the glasses targeted.

"A rower and a passenger," drawled the tall man in spotless white drill. "Recognize 'em, Pasqual?"

His companion grunted. "One of them, *señor*. The sleeper . . . Peeg Iron Jones."

The tall man lowered his binoculars. He was gray of hair and eyes and his high-boned face was as British as his bored voice. Yet a hint of inner excitement was glowing now in the depths of his cold eyes. He smiled thinly.

"Pig Iron Jones, eh? Our skipper . . . ?"

"Our skipper, *señor*. And, as I have told you, the hell of a tough baby."

11

Again their glances crossed. The tall Britisher was known in San Quentin as the *Señor* Tommy Atkins. His companion was none other than the notorious Pasqual Goldberg, self-styled mayor of the little town — the same Pasqual Goldberg who was reputed to have been the brains of half a dozen revolutions here and there between Chihuahua and Baja California. A small man, slight and dark and not yet out of his thirties, a man to reckon with in spite of his air of polite timidity.

"And the skipper's companion . . . ?" the *Señor* Tommy Atkins asked.

The Mexican shrugged. "*¿Quién sabe? A gringo,* per'aps."

"Some sort of crook," Atkins said slowly. "Honest men don't land at San Quentin from a smuggler's boat." His eyes narrowed. "Or perhaps, Pasqual, it's another of their spies." His brown hand touched the automatic that was slung in a shoulder holster beneath his white coat. "I suggest. . . ."

Pasqual Goldberg nodded. "*Sí, señor.* We go and see."

They walked at a leisurely gait toward the sleepy little town that lay under the lee of the cliff. The town of San Quentin, where many a sunny ocean lapped at a

white shore, where men came, like driftwood from unnamed places, to be alone
with the bitterness of their memories, to
drink themselves into forgetfulness, to fill
someday an unmarked grave. The haven of
forgotten men. Tommy Atkins, in his softer
moods, referred to San Quentin as a health
resort.

And now he and Pasqual Goldberg
strolled down into the town to have a look
at the fresh bit of human driftwood that
had been cast ashore. The skiff, with Jones
its sole occupant, was already on its way
back to the pseudo fishing boat.

The erstwhile passenger of the smug-
gling boat strolled up the dusty street, a
tall, splendidly built man of twenty-odd.
His clothes were well tailored but sadly out
of press. A month's beard was rudely
trimmed into Van Dyke pattern. The deep
bronze of wind and sun partly hid the
stamp of dissipation that reddened a pair
of blue eyes. He lugged an Army kit bag
and his gait was unsteady.

Only once during his walk up the street
did he betray the slightest interest in his
surroundings. That was when he passed a
board shack that bore a printed sign. His
bloodshot eyes studied the printing in
white letters against a sun-cracked black

background: **Pasqual Goldberg, Mayor**.

The man's bearded lips twisted into the semblance of a smile. Then, as if caught in some criminal act, the smile gave way to a straight-lipped line of bitterness. A moment later he stepped into the shadowy interior of a Mexican bar and ordered a quart of Scotch whiskey. Bottle and glass in hand, he sought a deserted table in a far corner, his kit bag between his feet.

He glanced up indifferently when Atkins and Pasqual Goldberg sat down at a nearby table a few minutes later. His eyes met those of the well-groomed Englishman, hardened into sullen defiance, then dropped to his glass of Scotch. He downed his drink in a single gulp.

Atkins approached his table and held out his hand. "Name's Atkins. Damn' glad to see a white man. Join us?" He nodded toward the table where Pasqual Goldberg was already ordering drinks from a grinning Mexican bartender.

The stranger looked up, suspicion in his glance. He made no offer to accept the Englishman's hand. "I'm about to get drunk, Atkins," he said, "and I'm rotten company when I'm drunk. I prefer being alone."

Atkins nodded shortly. "Bad habit, old chap, this one-man drinking. Know how you feel, though. Been there myself. Well, when you feel the need of companionship, the invitation stands open. *Adiós* . . . Captain."

The stranger was on his feet, upsetting his chair in the haste of his rising. He stood there, fists clenched, eyes burning. Atkins smiled and held out an open cigarette case.

"Easy, old chap. No offense meant. But when you erased the name on your kit bag, you did an incomplete job . . . left part of your rank visible. Have a cigarette?"

"Damn your cigarettes! And damn your prying insolence. For two-bits, I'd knock the smile off your conceited face."

"Two-bits? A quarter of a dollar in your American money, is it not? Righto." Atkins tossed a quarter on the American's table and, still smiling, faced the hot-eyed stranger.

The bearded man rushed, fists swinging. Atkins ducked, countered, and landed a clean blow to the American's jaw. Both showed science in their fighting. For weight and build they were not unevenly matched. But the Englishman's cleaner living threw the odds to his favor.

The fighting was swift, terrific, but clean. Then a left hook sent the American into the corner, a senseless heap. Atkins picked up his coat and turned to Pasqual Goldberg.

"Sober, he'd have thrashed me. Have the boys take him up to the house. Unless I'm badly mistaken, he'll join us. See that he's kept there until I come up."

Pasqual Goldberg smiled timidly and, with the assistance of two Mexicans, carried the unconscious American up the hill.

Back in a little room that adjoined the *cantina,* the *Señor* Tommy Atkins carefully and with thoroughness searched the service-worn kit bag. Then he repacked it and carried it up the cliff to the white adobe house of Pasqual Goldberg. A smile of satisfaction broadened the Englishman's lips as he climbed the slope. Pasqual Goldberg met him at the entrance to the large, shaded patio.

"*¿'Sta bueno?*"

"Rather. He's Captain Stuart MacLane of the Air Service. Dishonorable discharge. Woman in it somewhere. A dashed beautiful girl, from the ivory miniature in his bag. No letters or papers. Just that black discharge and the girl's face to keep him company. Poor devil. But, gad, what could be sweeter, eh? An aviator. Sent by Providence or the devil. But it'll take more than

16

three of us, what? Five's the right number,
I'd say. One million in gold divided among
five."

"Five." Pasqual Goldberg smiled his
apologetic smile and twisted a husk cigarette. "Five to start. But perhaps, *señor,*
not so many at the finish."

II

Stuart MacLane awoke. He lay on a bed covered by a Mexican serape. Beside him, on a table, stood a bottle and a glass. His head ached horribly and his jaw felt swollen and sore. He sat up, swung his legs to the floor, and reached for the bottle. He was alone in a white-walled room whose one iron-grilled window looked out across the sky-blue ocean.

Flooding back into his brain came the memories, black and bitter as quinine, memories of that one black day that stained a service record of spotless cleanliness. Court-martialed. Disgraced. . . .

He had taken it, standing at attention before a board of superior officers. Only his eyes had flinched under their verdict. After that he could not remember much except that he had gotten out of the room somehow, and out into the air. Dishonorably discharged from that Army to which he had given so much — stripped of his rank and his honor. Avoided by most of his brother officers, he walked down the squadron street. He wanted to be alone, but a man sat on his bunk, waiting for him. The man was hard-boiled, scar-faced Colonel Kirby, chewing a soggy cigar.

"They busted you, Mac?" Then, reading the answer in MacLane's eyes, he had ripped forth into a tirade that would have been rank anarchy had it come from any man but Kirby.

"Let 'em take their silver bars off you, Mac. Let 'em call you a thief or a yellow quitter or what they damn' please, old man. You and I know they lie. They've busted you. They've licked you with their damn' rules and regulations. But remember this, Mac. Don't ever forget it. I know that there's a nigger in your woodpile somewhere and you or no other man can tell me different. So wherever you go, whatever you do, don't lose your guts. Keep your head in the clouds, make a clean start somewhere, and forget about this man's army. Don't let this thing lick you."

And Kirby, hard-boiled Kirby, the fightingest fool of them all, had gripped his hand and then left him alone. None of the others had come near him. He had packed and gone away. The corporal had told him that Sergeant Conomy had not yet regained consciousness, that the doctors said there was only a slim fighting chance. So he had not gone to the hospital to see Sergeant Conomy, his passenger on that fatal flight that had landed the big, tobacco-chewing mechanic in the hospital and dragged Captain Stuart MacLane before a board of inquiry. He had gone away, not knowing whether Conomy would live or die.

For Stuart MacLane there had been no home to go to. He was glad of that, glad that his parents were dead. There had been just the girl. Just Betty Lou with her heart in her eyes as she held up her mouth to be kissed. Just her. But God, wasn't that enough? He wouldn't see her any more, ever.

So Stuart MacLane had avoided that little Virginia town and traveled on across the continent into Arizona. He had written her a letter, trying to explain why a daughter of an old Army officer could not possibly marry a man with a yellow discharge from that Army.

Lee Cartwright would tell her all the details. He'd been willing enough to testify at the hearing. He'd talked plenty about the wine at MacLane's birthday party the night before, about the smashed whiskey bottle in the wrecked ship. Then, later, about the squadron funds that were missing. Lieutenant Lee Cartwright had even suggested that the money had gone to furnish the wine and entertainment at the party. Oh, he'd tell Betty Lou the whole yarn, with trimmings. And he reckoned that someday she would marry Cartwright, whose old man had plenty of millions.

Arizona, then Mexico. Running away from his memories. From people. From the damnable black disgrace of it. San Quentin. Now he woke up with a swollen jaw and a headache and reached for the whiskey bottle.

As he did so, the door swung open and the Englishman strode into the room. MacLane scowled at him, then laughed shortly.

"You swing a mean left, Atkins."

"Couldn't have done it if you'd been sober, old boy. I hope you won't let the thing worry you." He found another glass and a soda bottle. "Might we drink a truce, old chap?"

"This is your liquor and your house," said MacLane. "I'd be a bum if I didn't. But from now on, lay off that captain stuff. Get me?"

"Perfectly. By what name do I address you?"

"Just Mac."

"Fair enough. Since this is neither my liquor nor my house, seems no more than proper that we should include our host. You have perhaps heard of Pasqual Goldberg?"

"Saw the name on a sign. Thought it was some sort of joke."

"Joke? Not at all. In our friend, the mayor of San Quentin, we have the rare affiliation of the Hebrew and the Castilian. An interesting combination." Atkins stepped to the door and called. A moment and the hook-nosed Pasqual was bowing his acknowledgment of the introduction.

"To a long and successful friendship," suggested Atkins.

"*¡Salud!*" Pasqual smiled.

"Here's how."

So began a partnership that was destined to be baptized in blood, baked beneath hot desert suns, and tried by the yellow gold lust. A partnership that was to bring death and success, that in the end was to bring forth the best and the worst in each man.

Perhaps the man who called himself Tommy Atkins visualized, in a measure, those things that were to come, for his eyes were on the blue sea and a whimsical smile twitched at his mouth under the closely trimmed gray mustache. A shadow of sadness clouded his eyes, filming them for a brief moment. He turned his face to MacLane.

"It is the *Señor* Goldberg's wish," he said pleasantly, "that you remain here as his guest. San Quentin has no inn of any sort, you know. You'll find us decent enough, each in his own way. Also, if you care to take a crack at it, there's a chance for you to clean up one-fifth share of a million in gold. Eh?"

"I don't get you, Atkins." MacLane stiffened, suspicion in his eyes. "I'm not as black as my appearance may lead you to believe. If it's running booze or hop, count me out, thanks."

"Quite so, old chap. But this is rather within the law, such as it is down in this country. Eh, Pasqual?"

"*Sí, sí, señor.* Hones' . . . *sí.* But dangerous, *sabe?* Per'aps the *Señor* Mac would not be so damn' 'appy to take the dangerous chance for that moch gol', no?"

"Dangerous, you say?" MacLane grinned crookedly. "Sound off with your proposition, gents."

Atkins and his partner exchanged a swift

23

look. Pasqual Goldberg smiled inanely and blew smoke from his nostrils. He had read into the heart of the American and touched the right chord of the outcast's emotions. The element of danger was more tempting than gold.

"Ees per'aps better, *Señor* Mac, to die of the bullet than of bad liquor, no?"

"You said it."

"If only," Atkins put in, "you could pilot an airplane!"

"You mean there's flying in it, Atkins?" Stuart MacLane's eyes were sparkling now.

"Flying? Rather."

"Then I'm your buzzard. Where's the ship?"

"Better let me put you the whole proposition first, old chap," suggested Atkins. "Then you take it or leave it. We ask only one thing. That is . . . keep your mouth closed. Just now, I'd advise a hot tub and a shave. Then meet us out in the patio."

Pasqual Goldberg and Atkins left the room. MacLane was alone. A Mexican brought in a huge wooden tub and filled it with buckets of hot water. MacLane dove into his kit bag for clean linen. Suddenly he straightened and his eyes narrowed. Someone had been searching that bag. Everything was there, but arranged differently. *Who . . . ?*

As if in reply to his question, the tall Englishman appeared in the doorway.

"It was I who went through your bag, MacLane," he said coolly. "Matter of precaution. The last American who blew into San Quentin was a damned spy. Tried to kill me one night. Mac, we don't give a good damn who you are, where you come from, or what you've done. I'm no white angel myself. But if I were you, I'd burn that damned discharge paper."

MacLane shook his head. "I don't know why I hang onto it, but I do."

"Confounded cheeky of me to paw over your luggage. But I had to be sure of my man. The game we're playing is hazardous. I think you'll like it. And I say, Mac, our friend, Pasqual, knows nothing of the paper. Better keep it on your person somewhere. A great chap, Pasqual, but . . . well, you understand, eh?"

"I get you, Atkins, and thanks. I'll be with you in half an hour."

III

It was dusk when Stuart MacLane, bathed, clean-shaven, dressed in breeches and boots, joined the two men in the patio. Below, in the calm bay that was opal-hued in the changing light of a Mexican twilight, the riding lights of fishing boats twinkled and winked saucily. Somewhere a woman played a guitar and sang softly to its accompaniment.

A dinner was already laid on spotless linen, out under the pepper trees. Candles shed a soft light on polished silver and cut glass. A Mexican *mozo* padded about on sandaled feet, serving drinks. Pasqual smiled as he noted the look of astonishment on the American's face.

"We are not so much the barbarian as you theenk, eh, *Señor* Mac?"

Later, as they were eating, MacLane noticed that guards paced up and down outside. Also, on top the flat roof, three more uniformed men squatted beside a machine-gun. He recalled Atkins's remark about the American spy and wondered for whom the man was spying and what had been his fate. He became more curious each moment regarding the expedition of which the Englishman had spoken. But it was only after the meal was done, and the servants had retired, that mention was made of it. When their cigars were going well, Atkins opened the subject.

"Ever hear of the Cartwright-Campbell Mining Company, Mac?"

MacLane started, hands clenching. He had sufficient reason to remember that company. For a year, while waiting his appointment to West Point, he had been an engineer for them. Moreover, old Martin Cartwright was the father of Lee Cartwright — Lieutenant Lee Cartwright whose testimony had damned MacLane in the eyes of a court-martial board.

"Yes," he replied coldly, "I've heard of the company."

"You knew they had holdings in Mexico?"

"Until the revolutions drove them back across the line."

"Exactly, old chap. Martin Cartwright began something that grew out of his power to handle. Cartwright money financed the first revolution in that state.

You didn't know that, I'll wager. Few Americans do. But it's the truth. Cartwright fancied he was paying the *jefe* of the state too big a percentage of his bullion, so he decided to put in power a less mercenary governor in place of the *jefe* who was bleeding him. Our friend, Pasqual, engineered the deal from start to finish. Hired gun-runners, recruited an army, carried on all negotiations between Martin Cartwright and a certain General Manuel Cortéz. Pasqual, in his own quiet way, is quite a king maker.

"A few thousand rounds of machine-gun bullets, a dead Mexican or two, a very dead *jefe,* and it was all over but the *vivas.* Martin Cartwright and his new governor met in El Paso and signed articles of agreement. As Pasqual puts it, everything was *'sta bueno.* That is, to all appearances. The devil of it was, the *gringo* Cartwright, for all his business ability, had fallen sadly short in his estimate of the new *jefe,* who, ignoring the papers signed in El Paso, demanded twice the tithe that Cartwright formerly paid. Rather a joke on the Cartwright-Campbell faction, eh?

"But the mines were rich and they kept on working. Each clean-up time, our worthy Governor Manuel Cortéz was

Johnny-on-the-spot to collect his percentage of the bullion. Cartwright cursed and fumed and appealed here and there to higher powers, who only shrugged fat shoulders.

"Then enters the third factor. This Manuel Cortéz is not too popular among his people. Strange to relate, a goodly portion of those machine-guns have become lost and have fallen into the hands of another rebel general. Odd, what? Perhaps friend Pasqual might explain that better than I? Eh, Pasqual?"

"*Sí.* Why not? Ees like thees. Thees *Señor* Martin Cartwright, just like I figure, ees hol' out that money wheech he promise' me. Ees one evil man of the extreme double-cross nature, that one. He forget about that money he promise' me an' send out word to the soldiers to shoot that damn' Pasqual Goldberg where they find heem. There, *Señor* Mac, ees where that *gringo* make the 'ell of a bad mistake." Pasqual smiled apologetically and lapsed into silence.

Atkins grinned at the moon and went on in a lazy voice: "So, with a fair-size army guarding the border, this Manuel Cortéz chap cannot slide his bullion across into the safe American territory. So what does he do? He buries it. Here and there, deep under the ground, each week's bullion gets planted. And that, as you say in America, is that. Except for the fact that Pasqual has a spy in camp who watches that gold get buried. Joke's on Cortéz, what?

"Then, about that time, Pancho Gutiérrez and his boys get playful and those other revolutions are child's play by comparison. The Cartwright-Campbell mines close down for keeps. Some drunken Mexicans burn the mill and the buildings. Today nothing remains but the ruins of some expensive machinery, some charred timbers, and the tailings dump."

"An' the one million dollars in bullion which that *jefe* Manuel Cortéz bury but gets shot against the wall before he can enjoy one dollar from it," put in Pasqual. "Ees time for one dreenk, no?"

They drank. Each man seemed wrapped in his own thoughts. It was MacLane who broke the silence.

"Does Cartwright know of this buried gold?"

"Rather, old chap. He's sent half a dozen expeditions down there. They dug up the country for miles. Once they nabbed Pasqual and tried to make him talk. That's where he and I met. I happened along about the time the blackguards were toasting his feet over a bed of red coals. Three of them . . . all white men, too. Being in the dark, I had the edge."

"Don't let the *Señor* Atkins fool you. Son-of-a-gon, how he fight! One agains' three, *Señor* Mac. *¡Caramba!* An' I am tie' an' cannot be of one damn' bit of the assistance weeth heem. Someday, my frien', I 'ave 'ope to pay you back for that night."

"Getting back to the subject," Atkins went on, "our job is to lift that gold and land it here at San Quentin. A distance, as the crow flies, of five hundred miles. You see where we could use a plane and a good pilot, Mac?"

"Sounds simple enough," said MacLane.

"Not so simple as it seems to sound. That country is overrun with chaps who want that gold. They don't know where it's buried. Pasqual knows. The spy who watched the stuff being buried knows."

"And where is the spy?"

"Ah, there you have the fly in the ointment, as it were. The chap vanished after he turned the map over to Pasqual. We have reason to believe that he made it across the border. His motive might be to seek safety. On the other hand, it might occur to him to sell his wares twice. In other words, interest Cartwright or someone else in this duplicate map which he perhaps carries with him."

"*Hmm.* Not so good. They might take a crack at it before we get there."

Pasqual grinned. "Ees bad mistake for them, een that case. My men guard that place. Tough *hombres,* them soldiers there."

"I told you Pasqual was long-headed." Atkins smiled. "What do you think of it all, Mac? Want to get in on it?"

"You can't keep me out of it." MacLane was on his feet now, straight-backed, clear-eyed, sober. Here was an outlet for the black memories that clogged his brain and heart.

"Ees time for one dreenk, no?"

"I'd rather not," replied MacLane. "I'm about caught up with the stuff, if you don't mind."

"Righto, old warrior." Atkins grinned. "Gad, you're a different-looking man than the wreck I knocked down. A week of swimming down in the bay, some decent food, and plenty of sleep, and you'll be fit as a cricket. Then we'll get that ship out of the crate and try her out, eh?"

MacLane nodded, his gaze fixed on the moonlit bay far below. He was thinking, just then, of Sergeant Conomy, of his last flight. Of the smashed whiskey bottle found in the wreckage. If only Conomy were there to assemble that plane. Conomy, who loved the game and who knew a ship from prop to tail skid. Conomy, to whose dusty ears the roar of a motor was music. Conomy, his flying mate who perhaps lay buried back there in an Army post grave. Was he Conomy's murderer?

MacLane wondered if his nerves would snap if he again took a ship off the ground. He had seen good pilots lose their innards like that. What had happened, anyhow, on that final flight? The crash had left him unconscious for hours. He recalled taking off that morning. He vaguely remembered the formation flight. Lee Cartwright, flying on his right, a recruit on his left. Kirby signaling for a zoom. His joy-stick wagging loosely in his hand. Or had it? Then nose down, headed for the earth that flew up to meet him. After that, oblivion. And the smashed whiskey bottle someone had found. Not his. Not Conomy's. Whose, then? Who had planted that smashed bottle in his wrecked cockpit?

MacLane swung about, facing Atkins and Pasqual Goldberg. His eyes were glinting with a hard light and his mouth was set in a grim line.

"I don't know whether it was the sock on

the jaw, or the dinner, or those lights down on the bay," he said, smiling queerly, "but something has given me a new perspective. I've been a quitter. I've done what Kirby warned me against. I lost my guts. Tonight I've got 'em back. I'll fly your crate to hell and back, and, when the job's done, I'm going back home and sift something to the bottom."

Atkins nodded. The Englishman was thinking of the ivory miniature he had seen in MacLane's kit bag.

"Great place, home," he said, staring across the moonlit ocean. He looked older, somehow, as he spoke. Again that wistful smile hovered about his mouth. "Might as well turn in and sleep, what?" He turned and walked away. Pasqual and MacLane were left alone.

"The braves' man I 'ave ever known," spoke Pasqual softly. "An' the most saddest. Me, I 'ave never been like that, in love."

"In love?"

"What else, *señor? Buenas noches.*"

And so Captain Stuart MacLane sought his bed. He dropped off to sleep with the distant smile of a Mexican love song lulling his weary brain and body.

IV

It must have been almost daylight when Stuart MacLane awoke, startled from profound sleep into wide-eyed wakefulness. He sat up in bed, peering about the room that was dark save for a strip of moonlight that came from the iron-grilled window. Without knowing why, he slipped from the bed and dug into his bag for his Army automatic. With the weapon in his hand he felt more secure. From outside in the patio came voices. One, calm, even-toned, coldly dangerous. The voice of the *Señor* Tommy Atkins.

"*¿Por que?* Who goes there?"

"Officers and soldiers of the federal army!" called a voice in English. "Open the gate."

"What is your business?"

"We have arrest paper for a Thomas Atkins."

"What charges?" Atkins's voice bit the silence like cold steel.

"Conspiracy against the government of

Mexico. Murder of three American citizens. Inciting rebellion among the Mexican people." The voice rasped harshly. "Open up or we'll blow this damn' shack off the map. There's a gunboat in the bay with her guns trained on this place."

"And just who might you be?" asked Atkins.

"That concerns me. If you're Atkins, better step out and surrender."

"Keep your bally shirt on, old chap. I'm not in the habit of surrendering." He snapped a couple of staccato questions in the Mexican tongue.

"*¡Sí, sí, señor!*" came the quick replies from the roof where the machine-gun was placed.

Stuart MacLane, gun swinging in his hand, slipped into the patio and would have crossed over toward the shadow beyond from where the voice of the Englishman came, only the hand of Pasqual Goldberg reached from a dark niche and touched his arm.

"Ees better to stay home, *señor*. The orders of *Señor* Atkins."

Atkins was again speaking, his voice now mockingly sarcastic.

"In case, *Señor Gringo,* that you did not understand the meaning of the questions I

36

addressed to my men, allow me to translate. I asked them if the machine-gun on the roof had you and your spies covered. They assured me that such was the case. The gate of the patio is a foot thick and the walls some twelve feet high. By the time you begin an assault, our Lewis gun will be playing 'God Save the King' on your vest buttons. As for your silly gunboat, you haven't a gunner that can hit the side of Gibraltar at point-blank range. I'll give you five minutes to take your tin soldiers and go home. My men need some moving-target practice, so don't tempt us too far. Vamoose, *gringo*. When you get home, tell Cartwright to try again."

Pasqual Goldberg chuckled softly. Mac-Lane made him out now, standing there in gaudy silk pajamas, a Luger in one hand, knife in the other. Gone was the apologetic smile and the soft eyes. Pasqual's face was sinister in its hardness and his eyes were black slits.

"Ees the 'ell of a bluff, eh, *amigo? Santa María,* the *Señor* Atkins ees brave man, no?"

From outside the patio wall came sounds of movement. Barked orders — a boatswain's whistle — the chatter of breech bolts. They were retreating. When the last sounds dimmed in the distance, Atkins came across the patio. He was fully clothed and armed with two single-action Colts guns.

He smiled grimly and lit his pipe. Here was the type of Britisher that held India and Africa by sheer nerve and splendid morale.

His voice was matter-of-fact: "Afraid you're in for it, Mac, unless you withdraw immediately. The Yank wasn't bluffing. There's a Mexican gunboat in the harbor. Cartwright has cut through enough red tape to get government backing. That means Pasqual and I are now outlaws with probably a price on our heads. You still have a chance to drop out before they return, old chap."

"I'll stick around, Atkins," replied MacLane. "I can use some excitement. You're the skipper. Sound off with the orders."

"Good. Can you ride a horse?"

"Raised on one."

"Splendid. Know machine-guns, of course?"

"Lewis, Vickers, and Colt."

"Fine. Get into some clothes. Pasqual, I have to separate you from those delightful pajamas, but you'll do better work clothed properly. Have some breakfast stirred up . . . horses ready. We'll give the black-and-tan chaps a little hot lead, then cut and run for it. Mac will man the gun on the right wing of the patio. I'll take the other. You tend to the horses and pack mules. The beggars came sooner than I anticipated. That means there's a traitor in camp. News has leaked out. Who was on sentry duty the past hour?"

"José Garcia."

"Find out why he didn't give the alarm when that boat dropped anchor. Why the invaders weren't challenged as they slipped up here. And lastly, Pasqual, find out why the patio gate was unbarred."

There was a quiet grimness in Atkins's voice that was chilling.

"*Santa María,* those gate unbarred, you say?"

"Absolutely. And had I not been alert, we'd have been murdered where we slept. Stop the leak, like a good chap."

Pasqual was off on a trot, muttering Mexican imprecations.

"Get into your boots and breeches, Mac. They'll be . . . ah, I thought so."

The boom of a gun came from down on the bay. The shell went wide.

"They'll waste some good shells getting

our range." Atkins smiled grimly. "Rotten gunners. Later, when the light's better, they may knock the dust off Pasqual's house. Then their bally marines and soldiers will attack. Our play is to keep them off until Pasqual gets a trail cut through the troops back in the hills. He and I have been virtually prisoners here for two weeks. But we've recruited quite a cavalry outfit while they had us cooped up. Ah!"

Atkins held up his hand in a gesture that meant silence. From somewhere beyond the patio came the rattle of breech bolts. A sharp command. Then a short volley.

"I would say, for an offhand guess, that Pasqual has found the traitor and stopped the leak. Now, old chap, slip into some clothes. Don't let the shelling upset your appetite. They won't find us until daylight. How do you like your eggs?"

"Eggs?"

"Breakfast, you know. Boiled or poached or perhaps fried?"

"Any way," replied MacLane dazedly. The calm of the Britisher was a little appalling. That volley had killed a man or several men. And almost in the same breath this Atkins spoke of eggs. He was still stunned as he washed and dressed. He could hear Atkins pacing about, whistling softly. Then a voice roared out of the quiet dawn.

"Ahoy, the house!"

No mistaking that roaring voice. A sailor's voice, carrying the salty heartiness of the open sea. The voice of one Pig Iron Jones, smuggler, modern-day pirate, the toughest skipper on the Pacific coast.

"Ahoy, the house!"

"Ah, Captain Jones." Came the clatter of gate bars, then a red-faced, bull-necked man in seaman's dungarees rolled across the tiled patio, directing his course toward a bottle of whiskey that stood on a moonlit table.

"Need a snifter, Atkins. A mile swim and the walk up that damned hill made me dry. To say no word of a scrap or two on the way. Those damned *cholo* gobs sunk the *Harriet Anne* and I had to swim for it. Here's health, Atkins. Swam, mostly underwater on account the damned fools were shooting at my head. Good licker, Atkins. Here's health. See anything of the drunken guy I beached this afternoon? Bird with whiskers and a bad hangover?"

"He's with us. One of us."

"Sized him up as all right, once he got sober enough. Game cuss. Sick as a cook's cat but never whined. Here's health. Got a

41

rag handy? They nicked my shoulder."

MacLane grinned as he pulled on his boots. His grin widened as he joined the two in the patio, and Jones blinked astonishment.

"You sure look different, mister. Knock me green if you don't shake off a jag quick. You can ship with me any time." Then recalling the sunken *Harriet Anne*, he ripped off a string of sailor's curses. Atkins and MacLane dressed a flesh wound in the skipper's shoulder while that salty gentleman drank the better part of a quart of Scotch without showing a symptom of intoxication.

"Ever ride a horse, Jones?" asked Atkins.

"Make it a bicycle and I'm your man. Horse? A wooden one, once, on a merry-go-round when I was a C.P.O. on the Mississippi. I might hold down the deck of a buggy if you tied a horse to it. I'm a sailor, not a cowboy."

"It will be slow riding," Atkins told him, "mostly mountains."

"I'll walk," announced Jones flatly. A bursting shell halted all conversation for the moment. Atkins whistled soundlessly.

"That's either an accident or they have a Yank gunner. That was close."

"They got a white guy findin' range.

Heard him givin' orders. Another white guy handlin' the gun. And there's somethin' phony about that boat. She ain't Mex."

"Eh?" Atkins spun about briskly. "Not a Mexican gunboat?"

"She's flyin' the greaser flag, but I'm tellin' ya she ain't a Mex boat. She's a subchaser. Small guns fore and aft, see. Manned by a pick-up crew of wharf rats from up the coast. She'll haul anchor before sunrise or I'm a landlubber. She's private-owned. Phony clearance papers from somewhere around Seattle, maybe. Runnin' guns down and runnin' hop back. Sounds goofy, but I'm layin' a bet some big guy buys her off some South American state for plenty jack." He downed another drink. "Now here she is. Blows my *Harriet Anne* into slivers and drops some hot ones on Pasqual's roof. Not so good."

"Nor so bad." Atkins smiled. "At least we're not bucking the Mexican government. Better take your post, Mac. Jones, locate Pasqual and tell him we're leaving at daybreak . . . gad, here they come!"

From the roof, a sentry called out. MacLane climbed to the machine-gun mounted on the right wing of the house that was built to enclose three sides of the open patio. The gun was on the roof and two nervous Mexicans were crouched behind a barricade of sandbags. MacLane took over the gun, examining with expert swiftness the magazines, firing mechanism, and tripod. The familiar feel thrilled him oddly.

Cutting up over the edge of the cliff was a moving blot that, once on the strip of mesa, scattered into deployed formation, advancing with caution, closer each moment, using rocks and brush patches for concealment. MacLane now perceived that the house of Pasqual Goldberg backed up against a deep barranca that could be entered only by means of a steep trail that led from that part of the house that was used for a storeroom. A trap door, perhaps, that led one down rock steps into the cañon below where brush and rocks hid the stables and corrals. A veritable fortress.

He dimly saw the approximate lay of the building and surmised the rest of it as he watched the crawling blots that came close across the mesas that stretched between the house and the edge of the cliff overlooking the town and bay.

A whistle shrilled. Then a score or more crimson flashes hit into the night as the invaders raked the roof with rifle fire.

Rat-tat-tat-tat-tat. A machine-gun was spitting, down there among the rocks, spraying deadly hail about MacLane's position.

"Fire at will, Mac!" called Atkins, and the Englishman's gun went into action. MacLane swung his muzzle on the nest of rocks that hid the enemy gun, and the next moment the Lewis was raking the spot. A Mexican, squatted beside MacLane, leaped in the air, screaming, then crumpled in a heap.

The second Mexican, muttering profanity and prayer, handed the American a fresh magazine, then slid from the roof into the safety of the patio. MacLane was left alone.

His gun jammed and the correction of the jam took precious minutes. Then he went into action again, slashing the ground below with a raking fire. The enemy machine-gun was quiet and only the rifles were going. Now and then a groan or curse or a threshing body in the brush indicated a hit. After some time — perhaps half an hour — the whistle screeched again. Guns went silent. The enemy was retreating. The finger of dawn marked the ragged skyline in the east.

"Ahoy, Atkins!" Jones swung on sea legs

across the patio toward the bottle on the table. "Pasqual says he's ship-shape and ready to haul anchor. Hell, the bottle's empty. When do we eat?"

"Tonight, Jones. No breakfast now. The land forces are retiring. That means they'll shell us in about fifteen minutes. Pasqual get a trail open at the mouth of the barranca?"

"He did and no foolin'. But he can't hold it open long, he says. Better rattle our timbers before the light gets good."

"Righto. I say, Mac, are you fit?"

"Sitting pretty."

"Wreck your gun and come on, then. We're about to sound retreat. Those Johnnies have our range, I think. There's a bottle of acid beside your gun. Pour it down the barrel. Then hop down and we'll join Pasqual below."

MacLane found the acid. Its contents sizzled down the hot barrel and thus a good gun was put out of commission. Then he slid down the ladder into the patio and joined Atkins and Jones. The latter had armed himself until he fairly bristled with guns.

"Hit, Mac?" questioned Atkins. "No? Splendid. Open the trap, Jones. That's the ticket." He switched on an electric torch and MacLane saw a seemingly endless flight of stone steps that dropped into the black maw below.

"Careful, now. Here's another pocket flash. One step and it'll take a vacuum cleaner to pick you up off the cañon floor. Jolly place, what?"

And so they dropped down into the barranca below. Pasqual met them. The fellow smiled a greeting, then led the way to a corral where saddled horses moved restlessly.

"Don't think much of our Mexicans, Pasqual," said Atkins. "Mine quit me when it got hot. How about your crew, Mac?"

"One got killed. The other ran."

"*Sí,*" agreed Pasqual apologetically. "But I do not keel them. In the bush, on a horse, they are *muy bravo*. But not, *señores,* on top of the house roof. Me, I am like that myself. So I should not keel a man for doing what me myself personal would do. You *sabe?*"

"Perfectly, old boy. The mule is for Jones?"

"For the *Señor* Jones. Ees damn' good mule. Sit on him and he weel take you places. But be careful you do not lay the 'and on hees neck. He ees train' mule. Weeth the 'and on hees neck, he bock."

47

"I'm takin' my voyage afoot," said Jones grimly. "I ain't no mule rider."

"Try some of this," suggested Atkins, passing over a black bottle. "Then you'll beg us for a bronco to tame."

V

From the mesa above came the muffled thud of shells that were wrecking Pasqual's house. Ahead lay the brush-choked barranca with its twisting trail that led inland into the mountains. From somewhere came the rattle of rifle fire. Pasqual shrugged slim shoulders and cast a speculative eye at the rose-hued dawn that crept across the sky.

"Ees not so damn' good, thees daylight, eh, *caballeros?*"

"Might be worse." Atkins smiled.

"Not for me," groaned Jones, hanging to the saddle horn. "How the hell can I put up a scrap when it takes both my hooks to stay aboard this animal?"

"Where's that ship, Atkins?" asked MacLane.

"Inland from here, Mac . . . Black Agate Mesa, level as a table for a mile. I wish we could have bought a newer, better ship, but we had to take what was offered. Had the devil's own time getting it there by mule back, but we managed. The fuselage was the worst. Bulky, y'know. Trail twisting up the mountainside. Had to travel by night. Killed five mules and a Mexican or two negotiating the curves. But we made it."

They rode on. The firing became more distinct as they approached the mouth of the long barranca. Atkins and Pasqual rode side-by-side. Behind them came MacLane and the muttering Jones.

"All right, men!" called Atkins presently. "Get ready for the race. Ride hard and shoot to kill. They'll be at us from all sides. Our men will fall in behind us as we go. They're hidden all along here. You can't see 'em but they're here. Stop for nothing. All set? Let's go!"

They shoved their horses to a swift lope. Then, like a hailstorm, bullets sprayed the rocks. Atkins and Pasqual shooting as they led the way. MacLane quirting Jones's mule. The terrific clatter of gunfire. Excited orders from the rocks — Mexican orders. A machine-gun clattered death warning from ahead until Atkins, with the courage of a man gone mad, charged his horse up the slope and, before the gun could riddle him, silenced the gun crew with his two Colts. He came back, loading, as his horse leaped and slid down the in-cline. His face was set in a grim smile. Pasqual was jabbering and shooting as he leaned across the neck of his horse.

MacLane, pale but dangerously calm under fire, stayed close by the unfortunate Jones, who was hard put to keep his seat on the racing, dodging mule. The seaman swore hastily and tried an occasional shot as the mule tore on in the wake of Pasqual's horse. Then the doughty skipper of the sunken *Harriet Anne* forgot the warning and clutched the mule's neck. The next moment he was rolling among the rocks. The mule kept going, braying after the horses ahead.

MacLane jerked his horse to a halt. Jones got to his feet, swearing.

"Up you come, Jones. Behind me. Snappy, man!" MacLane pulled him up behind his saddle and started. Twenty feet ahead the trail was blocked by a swarm of villainous-looking Mexicans who were shooting excitedly, yelling the while.

"Sit tight, Jones. Shoot fast. We're off!" They charged into the midst of the Mexicans, who gave way before the attack. Jones was shooting now, a gun in each hand, keeping his precarious seat with no little difficulty.

Something hot seared MacLane's cheek.

The horse stumbled, went to its knees, then was up again as Jones gripped his companion in a bear-like hug.

Then they were on a clear trail again, racing in the wake of Pasqual and Atkins, who had halted when the mule caught up to them.

"What I tol' you about that mule?" yelled Pasqual. "Ees trick mule!"

Jones groaned and held onto MacLane with a death grip. "Lemme walk, that's all. Lemme walk."

"The first hundred miles are the hardest, Skipper." MacLane grinned, recalling Jones's remark when he had been so seasick on the *Harriet Anne*.

"This evens us, Mac." Jones got the point. "And listen, mate, you saved my neck. I ain't forgettin', see."

They left the barranca behind. When they were well beyond the danger zone, Atkins called a halt.

"We'll wait here for the men. Those beggars don't dare follow us out into the open country. Wish I could have stayed back with the boys, but we four, as the leaders of this expedition, must not take any needless risks. Our men are ably commanded, eh, Pasqual?"

"*Sí, sí.*" Pasqual chuckled and Atkins

grinned as if they enjoyed some joke between them.

"You haven't met our general, Mac. Wait until you see him. I'll wager you'll be glad you came. He's worth seeing. And fight? He's an army in himself, our general. Listen. Hear him?"

From back along the trail came the clatter of a cavalry troop on the double quick. But above the rattle and clanking came a voice: "Column of fours, you boneheads! Fours, can't you savvy? *Uno, dos tres, cuatro!* Column of *cuatros,* you fleabit, marijuana-smokin' sons-of-hydrophobia-polecats! Column of *cuatros,* and make it snappy! Ramón, Pedro, Sanches, Herrera! What the hell ya think I made ya corporals for? Oh, you babies! Oh, you fatheads! *Cuatros,* dammit!"

"That," announced Atkins proudly, "is our general. I say, Mac, what's wrong?"

"Wrong?" MacLane's voice was a husky, croaking sound. "Wrong? My God, man, nothing's wrong. It's *right!*" And whirling his horse, he raced back along the trail.

At the head of a struggling, motley-clad but splendidly accoutered troop of native cavalry rode a white man. A ragged, red-faced giant of a fellow astride a roan mule. Perspiring, one cheek bulging with tobacco, a campaign hat cocked rakishly over one eye. About his middle were two heavy cartridge belts. On each thigh hung a big Colt.

MacLane slid his horse to a halt.

"Conomy!" he croaked.

"The devil save us! Cap MacLane!" The rider of the roan mule halted so abruptly that his followers all but rode him down.

"Halt!" barked the red-faced commander. "Halt, you boneheads! Captain Mac! Am I dreamin'? Mitt me, Cap! Mitt me an' tell me I ain' gone goofy. By the jumpin', runnin' devils uh good luck, I'm glad to see ya, Cap."

"Sarge! Conomy, old boy! Conomy." There were tears in the eyes of MacLane as his hand was crushed in the hairy paw of the man that he thought dead. "They said you were dying, Conomy. And . . . I . . . I. . . ."

"You done the only thing you could do, Cap. Me die? With two months' pay comin'? Not Kid Conomy. Say, I bin all over hell an' back, huntin' you. Lost your trail in Arizona. Talk about luck! Talk about . . . hey, there, you pack uh bean-eatin' bums, column uh *cuatros*. Come on, Cap, we gotta keep movin' or these babies'll bush up on me an' go ta sleep. I got four hitches in the U.S. Army in every branch from signal corps to cavalry, but I never seen their beat. Column uh *cuatros,* you tar babies. We'll eat when we get there, so come on. I know where there's a tequila still near camp. Atta babies." Conomy winked at MacLane. "See how they perk up when I say tequila? Yeah, bin huntin' all over for ya."

"For me? Why?"

"Kirby's orders. Colonel Kirby."

"What?"

"Sure." Conomy spat at a rock and grinned. " 'Conomy,' says Kirby when I was mustered out, 'go find Captain MacLane wherever he is. I want him. Draw on me for whatever you need. Don't come back till you bring Mac with you.' "

"What's the idea?"

"Search me, Cap. He didn't say. Him an' some dame has a long powwow, see. Just before the colonel come into all that money and resigned. She was weepin' all over his Croix de Guerre. She all but kissed me when I said I'd find you if it took the rest of my life. She's with Lieutenant Cartwright and some old boy with whiskers. I kinda got it that Old Whiskers is Cartwright's old man, see."

MacLane, a little white about the lips,

took a leather case from his coat pocket and opened it.

"Was this . . . was this the girl, Sarge?"

"That's her, Cap! A pippin', if I ain't too fresh in sayin' so. She never bats an eye when Kirby cusses over some letter she hands him. By the way he talked, I think he's gonna crucify ya when he catches ya, Cap."

Conomy again turned his profane attention to his grinning troop of fighting Mexicans. By the time he had them again in some sort of formation, they had reached the spot where Pasqual, Jones, and Atkins were waiting. Conomy threw them a salute and barked his outfit to a halt.

This cavalry commander was a different Conomy than MacLane had known in the service. He faced Atkins, who returned his salute stiffly.

"General Conomy reports twenty-eight dead and five missing. The rest all present. Following Major Atkins's orders, we took no prisoners."

This mock-military business should have been ludicrous but somehow MacLane could find nothing humorous in it. The Mexicans were impressed by the formality of the white men, that was plain. Pasqual Goldberg sat his horse with the stiff back of an officer. Yet MacLane sensed a hint of sly humor beneath the stiffness of Atkins and Conomy. As if they were playing at some amusing little game. Yet there was blood and dust and powder smudges that gave mute evidence of the seriousness of that same game. A game of life against death.

"Put your men at rest, General," said Atkins.

"Company, 'tention! Rest! Hey, dammit, don't fall out! Rest means smoke. *¡Cigarros, hombrecitos!* Atta babies! Sufferin' snakes, what a outfit!" He reached for papers and tobacco and grinned at Jones.

"Well, if it ain't the skipper! H'are ya, Pig Iron?"

"Damn' near dead."

"The old fish outta water, eh? You ain't seen the half of it, Jonesy."

Atkins was looking from MacLane to Conomy, a peculiar smile on his mouth.

"I say, you two chaps seem to be acquainted," he spoke carelessly.

"Acquainted? You said it." Conomy grinned. "Him an' me won the war together, eh, Cap? Old buddies. You sure got a pilot for that ship now, Major. I was willin' to take a crack at it, but for all I've had more hours in the air than the average

57

eagle, I'm a lousy pilot. I can sure set one up on her nose. Two-point landin's is my specialty. But next to Colonel Kirby, Cap MacLane is the sweetest pilot that ever sat in a cockpit. And a bunch uh damn' keewee, pot-bellied majors busts him. Say, Cap, I got somethin' to say when we get home. I got a hunch who that rat was that put that hooch in our ship. He's the same baby that filed the control wires. . . ."

"Chop it, Conomy." MacLane's tone was sharp. Then, seeing the crestfallen look on Conomy's red face, MacLane smiled. "Don't reckon it makes much difference, Sarge, only I'm a bit touchy. After all, Atkins and Pasqual and Jones don't give a damn if I'm a blackbird. You say you know who planted the bottle in our ship?"

"I ain't sure. Just a hunch, that's all. Remember Sergeant Cline?"

"Cartwright's mec?"

"The same baby." Conomy turned to Atkins. "Remember the day I blew into San Quentin with Jones? I ask about a guy with a red scar across his left cheek? You shut up like a dumb oyster until you see I'm right, then you tell me he blows the burg after he tries to knife you an' don't aim right?"

Atkins nodded. "The blighter got away."

"Yeah. An' Kid Conomy joined up with

you in hopes of someday meetin' up with that same bozo, though I don't tip my hand, see. Jonesy knew. Him an' me was *muy amigos* over in the Philippines an' I could trust him, see. So when Jonesy says stick around, I does it. That's once that salty son-of-a-sea-horse was right."

"I say" — Atkins smiled — "quite a family gathering, what? Small world and so on. But we're wasting time. General Conomy, can you persuade your army to move on a few miles?"

"Watch me, that's all." He turned to MacLane. "I'm rankin' officer down here, Cap. Them babies don't savvy nothin' under a general, see. But Major Atkins is the real skipper." He turned to his rag-tag cavalry, who had dismounted and were squatting in the meager shade, smoking or tying rags about ugly-looking wounds.

"Up on your dead feet, *hombrecitos! Pronto!* You there, Sergeant, tell 'em in Mex. Make it snappy or I'll bust you, see? *Arriva* the mules! Hit the grit! Pull your ears in an' wipe off your chins! Make them eyeballs click! Forward, 'arch!"

The cavalcade rattled into motion.

Jones and Conomy rode side-by-side. MacLane, Atkins, and Pasqual Goldberg led the way. A scouting party under a gray-haired Mexican swung out of line and trotted off ahead, acting as advance guard and scouts.

The sun became hotter each hour. Ahead lay a ragged fringe of blue peaks. The Mexican troopers were singing a marching song that had a fascinating swing to its time. Cigarettes were rolled and lighted. Stuart MacLane was getting his first taste of Mexican soldiering.

He was also busy with a turmoil of thoughts. Conomy, alive and down in Mexico. Kirby and Betty Lou. Cartwright mixed up in this gold. Cline and the whiskey bottle. Fate seemed to be stirring up a concoction that was more than bewildering. How would it all end? Would the snarled skein untangle itself? Or would death ring down the curtain on the little drama?

VI

A white-hot sun blazed out of an azure sky, merciless and unceasing. The men grew silent under its grueling torture. Horses, their sweaty bodies dried and dust-caked, hit a dogged gait. Across miles of desert, sprinkled with Joshua trees, cactus, and mesquite. Then into the rough country clotted with ironwood and runty junipers.

There was wild game in abundance. Deer, sheep, goats, turkey, and quail. Then they came abruptly upon a crystal-clear creek that roared down out of a granite mountainside. Here they halted a few hours. Saddles were stripped from gaunt-flanked horses and mules. Packs were unloaded. Fires sprang into being and a meal was thrown together. Coffee, meat, and tortillas, but to MacLane it was a feast fit for the gods.

He and Conomy, their inner being satisfied and with cigarettes lit, sat apart from the others, talking in low tones. They had much to discuss, and, as Conomy talked,

Stuart MacLane listened with ever-growing interest.

"What you tell me, Conomy," said MacLane, "sounds darn' far-fetched. I never had much use for old Cartwright, but I never suspected him to be the scoundrel you paint him. Lee and I grew up together in the same little town. Cartwright practically owned the village. Stores, bank, light plant, and so on. We thought he made it out of his mines."

"Part of it, Cap. But only part of it. I ain't no lily-of-the-valley, see. I bin around and my playmates was sometimes kinda on the bum side uh the law, get me? A few times, when I'm kinda broke, I took a crack at bootleggin' an' what not. I run guns acrost this border more than once between El Paso and San Diego. So I pick up little bits of information, see. Stuff I keep mum about. Names of guys that travels among the high mucky-mucks. Sassiety gents with plenty dough that's in on the big deals. Runnin' booze, hop, and guns.

"Them babies is the brains an' the money back of the big deals. An' I'm tellin' ya, Cap, old Cartwright is the kingpin uh the works. That's the way he's piled up a lot uh jack that his home folks thinks comes from mines an' oil fields an' what not, see. He's the main gaffer of the smugglin' ring an' has bin for a long time. He's slick as a eel, crooked as a snake, an' tough as a bull hide. And Lee Cartwright is a chip off the old block. The old man's top kicker, now that he's outta uniform. Lee's a smooth baby. Plays this sassiety game to the limit. He don't take much chances, neither. Once in a while he gets into a tight and, when he does, watch him. He'll get you from behind. Sneaky scrapper, they say.

"This Cline gent is another baby that makes snake tracks when he travels. Lee passes the buck to Cline mostly. Cline slips it to one of his boys unless it's a ticklish job like croakin' Tommy Atkins. Oh, the Cartwright gang is a slick spread. Usta be Cartwright an' Campbell. Then Campbell gets took for a ride one night, down Los Angeles way. The bulls find his body next mornin' so full uh lead they can scarce lift it. Nobody never found out who done it.

"Campbell's interest goes to his partner, bein' this Campbell ain't got no heirs. An' I got plenty reason to know that Campbell was dead scairt of Cartwright. They're a nest uh snakes, Cap. We got 'em stirred up plenty. It's gonna be a sweet show before it's over. Hope Lee an' Cline cut in on it.

It'll be just too damn' bad if somethin'
happens to them two bozos. But first, Cap,
we're gonna put 'em through a course uh
sprouts an' find out the how-come uh that
smashed whiskey bottle an' that squadron
dough that turns up missin'. Say, if ol' man
Kirby knew what was comin' off, you
couldn't keep him outta Mexico with an
army. There's a sure real guy, Kirby. Plenty
dough an' a real friend. Millionaire, to
boot."

"Where is he now, Conomy?"

"New York, mebby. Mebby El Paso. Or
San Francisco. Or playin' polo with the
Del Monte swells. Hard ta say. His yacht's
off the California coast, I know that much.
Ready to shove off any time fer any place."

"He knows you're down here?"

"Man, his orders sent me here. When I
lose your trail, I take up Cline's, see. Playin'
both ends against the middle. Unless I'm a
bum guesser, Kirby had his own personal
reasons fer wantin' to smash Cartwright.
Somewhere, sometime, Cartwright done
Kirby dirt an' our colonel ain't the kind that
turns the other side uh his jaw ta get
slapped, get me? He's after Cartwright's
scalp. An' he sure likes you, Cap."

MacLane nodded, smiling twistedly. "I
know, Conomy. And I acted like a yellow

dog. Lost my guts."

"Lost nothin'," snorted Conomy. "Ferget it."

"God lets a man have but few friends," said MacLane musingly. "He's given me you and Kirby."

"How about Pasqual an' Atkins an' Jones?" Conomy grinned.

"I don't even know them well."

"Mebby not. But I do. Well enough to know that any of 'em will fight to the finish for any of the others. Pasqual's a half-breed Mex. Atkins is an outcast from home, an' Jones is a smuggler. But they're right an' don't forget it. They'll tell you, down here in Mexico, that Pasqual Goldberg is a double-crossin' snake. But they lie. He fights 'em with their own kind uh weapons an' licks 'em. Atkins stands flat-footed an' fights in the open like his breed uh Englishman always fights. Givin' odds, smilin' that give-a-damn smile uh his, cool as a cucumber on ice. He was a battalion commander durin' the war. Kirby met him an' recognized him. He's Lord Somebody or another. Soldiered in Africa and India. Some scandal sent him here. But no cleaner scrapper ever spit in the devil's eye.

"As for Jones, he'll fight anybody any place with any kind uh weapons. And rules don't mean nothin' to that gent. Bite, gouge, kick, knife, or shoot. An' he asks no favors when he's gettin' the short end of the bet." He grinned again. "Look at him now."

Pig Iron Jones was lying on his stomach, swearing gently but fervidly at mules and one mule in particular. Now and then he took a swig at the bottle at his elbow.

"How they comin', Jockey Jones?" called Conomy.

"I'm ruined, if that's what you're askin'. If I ever set foot on the deck of a ship again, I'll never take no shore leave. Drink?"

"Don't mind if I do." Conomy slipped a cud of tobacco from his cheek.

"Then go down to the creek an' drink your fill, ya big stiff." Jones chuckled, and drained the bottle. Conomy joined in the laugh that followed. Then he wagged a forefinger at Jones and spoke.

"That kills the bottle, don't it? An' where's the next comin' from? Listen, Jones, old sea dog, Kid Conomy knows where there's a nice tequila still goin' day an' night. About dark we'll be near there. You'll be wantin' a shot uh cactus juice to take the aches outta your bones. An' I ain't gonna tell ya where to snag a bottle. Laugh at that one, ya red-necked booze-hound."

"Aw, listen, Conomy, ol' shipmate, me 'n' you is. . . ."

"Is strangers that pass in the night, sweetheart. You ain't throwin' no lip over my bottle. An' between here an' camp, the country's all slants. You won't have a inch uh hide on ya that won't crave inside soothin' syrup."

Atkins had been sweeping the surrounding hills with his glasses and the big Englishman looked grave and a little worried. The others glanced up at him.

"Nothing alarming." He smiled reassuringly. "But I'd advise a double scout detail from here on. We're being watched from several points." He picked up a high-powered rifle that lay nearby. "Watch that back dot near the white rock on the mountainside." He adjusted the sights to a 500-yard range, took a rest across a tree limb, then pulled the trigger. The distant black dot leaped into the air. The faint echo of a man's scream drifted into silence. "Sniper." Atkins ejected the empty shell from the gun. "He might have been good enough to pick one or two of us off as we rode along the trail below him. There will be more scattered around up there, so keep a watch for them. I'd suggest waiting till dark, but the trails are too bad to travel by night, and, besides, we're undoubtedly being chased. So we'll run their bally gauntlet. Let's go."

"Listen!" It was Conomy's voice, husky with excitement, that threw a pall of silence over them. Conomy was looking at MacLane, smiling oddly as he cocked his head sideways. Then they all heard it. The drone of an airplane motor.

They waited, eyes sweeping the cloudless sky. Minutes passed. The droning hum became plainer. Then a dot showed above the hills, became more distinct, then took shape against the blue background. The ship circled the hills, swinging lower and lower.

"Scout plane," grunted Conomy.

MacLane nodded. "Steel guys instead of cables. Hums like a giant hornet. Look, Sarge, they've spotted us. He's sliding down for a look."

The plane came out of the heavens at a steep glide, leveled off, then circled back. The roar of the motor echoed across the hills. The ship with its two occupants tore past, not 200 feet above their heads. Two helmeted heads peered over the side. Then the ship zoomed and climbed back into the sky. The pilot banked sharply on a turn, swung the nose skyward, and headed back in the direction of San Quentin.

"Well, I'll be damned," grunted Atkins, breathing a heavy silence. "Checkmated, what?"

Conomy looked at MacLane, who stared after the vanishing ship with narrowed, flinty eyes.

"I was Lee Cartwright's instructor for a while," MacLane said as if musing aloud. "I've watched him from the ground too often to miss those little faults when he levels off and banks. That was Lee Cartwright at the stick of that ship."

"Notice them machine-guns, Cap?" added Conomy.

"I did," snapped MacLane, his voice hardening. He turned to Atkins. "What kind of a ship am I booked to fly?"

"A bomber."

The two flyers exchanged looks that spoke volumes.

"A bomber," said MacLane in a barely audible tone. "And he's piloting a scout plane with two guns. He can sit on our tail and play 'Yankee Doodle' on our backbones."

VII

"Well, Sarge" — MacLane voiced the question as they camped that night among the jagged peaks that pierced a moonlit sky — "what do you make of it?"

"Two and two makes ten." Conomy grinned. "Lee Cartwright an' Cline spots us today. We've tipped our hand an' there's gonna be some dirty fightin' before we lift that gold."

MacLane nodded grimly. "Wish we had that crate put together."

"You said a jaw full, Cap. The Black Agate Mesa is only half an hour from here by mule. Say we ride up there for a look at the crate?"

"Just what I was thinking. Sooner we start, the quicker we're done. It'll be the devil's own job with no hangar equipment, assembling that ship. Atkins says it's a bomber."

Conomy shrugged. "An old-time Army crate, from what I gathered," he said. "Gun turret. Rear cockpit has a stool for the gunner. Gun mounted on a circular track. Empty, we might give friend Cartwright a run for his jack. But loaded, we're not so good."

"Let's ride over, then."

MacLane found Atkins and told the Englishman their intentions.

"Better take some men along, Mac. Feel a bit uneasy?"

But MacLane shook his head. "I'll need Conomy to help assemble her. We'll need a light block and tackle to handle the motor. Tools to work with. Gas, oil, and water."

"Everything's there. Camouflaged with black canvas, the color of the mesa formation. Piñon trees for shade. A good spring nearby."

"Can you spare Conomy for a few days?"

"We can't, but we will, Mac. Pasqual and I, with Jones along, can hold our end. Also guard the one trail leading up there."

"Good." MacLane smiled. "Then Conomy and I will take along rations for a three-day stay up there. We'll be ready to take off by then."

"Splendid, Mac, old boy. Then you take off, land at a spot where we've more men planted, and wait there for ten days. That will give us time to make Sierra Blanca by forced marches. Sierra Blanca and Poison Wells are where the gold is buried. Conomy has a map of the country. Not a detail map, but I think you can navigate by it. There's a machine-gun cached beneath a ledge fifty paces to the west of the crated ship. Also a case of ammunition. The works are wrapped in oiled silk. There's also a cache of rations. I'm telling you this in case something pops and we get separated for any length of time."

MacLane grinned. "Conomy and I can get by all right."

Atkins nodded half-heartedly. "Suppose so, Mac. You'll find signal rockets, heliograph, and an electric flash for night signals. Morse code. Well, old man, wish you the best of luck."

MacLane gripped Atkins's hand, and joined Conomy, who brought the horses and ration kits. A moment later, after a brief farewell to Jones and Pasqual, the two rode off into the night.

The former sergeant seemed to know the country and led the way up a winding trail. Twice they were halted by guards and allowed to pass only when they were recognized. At the foot of the mesa they were again halted.

"Who goes?" rasped a voice in the Mexican tongue.

Conomy, in the lead, gave reply: "Friends."

"Countersign?" barked the Mexican.

"Rosarita," snapped Conomy.

MacLane stiffened in his saddle and reached for his gun. Conomy, for some reason, had not given the proper countersign!

"Pass, *amigos*." The guard stepped aside. Conomy rode boldly ahead. Abreast of the guard, Conomy leaned swiftly in his saddle. His six-shooter barrel crashed with a sickening thud on the guard's head. The man went down without a sound.

Conomy and MacLane slid from their saddles with one accord.

"Something wrong here, Cap," whispered Conomy. "This guy is one of Cartwright's *paisanos*. Suspected him when he challenged us. When he passed us on the wrong countersign, I knew I was right." Conomy dove into the brush and dragged out a Mexican, bound and gagged. His knife severed the ropes that bound the fellow.

"*¿Qué hay, hombre?*" whispered Conomy.

"Enemy, *Señor* General."

"Beat it for camp, then. Tell Atkins I

73

sent you. Tell him the enemy is close by. Vamoose . . . *pronto!*"

"*¡Sí, señor, sí!*"

"Beat it." Conomy turned to MacLane. "Well, Cap, do we go on up the trail?"

"Why not?"

"That's my sentiments." The big sergeant grinned. "Keep your eyes skinned and your gat handy. She's a steep climb, but I think we better go on foot. Won't make such a plain target. We'll crash the gate an' look over the situation on top, eh?"

MacLane nodded. "Suits me, Sarge."

Conomy was naturally assuming leadership, and rightfully. He knew the country, the people, and their methods of fighting. MacLane was content to abide by the big fellow's decisions.

Slowly, laboriously they climbed the trail. Now and then a rock slid from under their boots and betrayed their approach. Halting, getting their wind, straining every faculty to detect any presence of a lurking enemy, they negotiated the trail. When the rim of the lava mesa was skylighted against the pale, moonlit heavens, Conomy halted.

"Don't like this stillness, Cap. Lay all bets there's a few gents waitin' fer us on top. A deaf man could uh heard that last rock we jarred loose. All set?"

"Rarin' to go, Sarge," came MacLane's cool reply.

"Then here's at 'em." Conomy's voice broke into a loud shout: "Come on, babies! Eat 'em up, boys!" He charged up the hill, MacLane now abreast of him. "Charge 'em, *hombrecitos!*"

MacLane, getting the idea, added his yells to Conomy's. From above came confused orders. Sounds of near panic. Then Conomy's gun roared and MacLane shot at the vaguely moving blots above.

Sounds of cursing from above. Good American cuss words. Then the two invaders were in the midst of a milling bunch of Mexicans, who scrambled and shot wildly.

The guns of the two Americans blazed again and again into the mob.

"Surrender, *hombres!*" Conomy's yell was full of triumphant victory.

"*¡Socorro! ¡Socorro! Por Dios,* we quit!"

"Quit, eh, you damned yellow . . . *ugh!*" The speaker grunted as MacLane rushed him, gun empty, but still effective as a club. The heavy weapon felled the man.

"Surrender, *hombres!*" Conomy bawled harshly, and shot at a charging man, who screamed and ran backward, holding onto a wounded arm.

"We surrender, we surrender, *señores!*"

"Then drop your guns and knives. *Pronto!*" Conomy was charging here and there, clubbing guns from brown hands, hitting, smashing, bullying the frightened Mexicans into pitiful submission. "Gotta treat 'em rough," he panted, as they lined up a dozen or more prisoners. "Only methods these devils *sabe*. Where's the *gringo,* Mac?"

"Sleeping. Got these birds in hand, Sarge?"

"You bet."

"Then I'll take a look at the white guy." MacLane, puffing, sweating, a gun swinging in either hand, found his way to the spot where the unconscious American lay. He tied him securely and snapped a flashlight into the man's face.

"Know him, Cap?" called Conomy.

"Never saw him before. But he's a tough-looking specimen." He snapped off the light and joined Conomy. "What'll we do with these prisoners?"

Conomy grinned. Then he addressed the prisoners in a jargon of Mexican and pidgin English. Finally he found one among them who could interpret and so made clear his meaning.

"Double the pay you're getting, savvy? Plenty tequila. Plenty grub. Who joins General Kid Conomy? Tell 'em that I give 'em their choice, see. Join my outfit or I shoot 'em myself here an' now. Which is it, *hombrecitos?*"

"*Viva el general!*" came the ready chorus. There was no question as to their sincerity.

Conomy grinned at MacLane. "Not such a bad night's work, eh, Cap? Just the same, we keep their artillery for a while. These babies has changeable minds." He again addressed the interpreter. "Any more uh you men up here on the mesa?"

"No more, *señor*. Thees *gringo* say thees many men ees plenty to guard the trail. *Caramba,* he's the damn' liar, no?"

"Sure. How many men down below?"

"Wan honderd, per'aps, *señor*."

"How many Americans among 'em?"

"Ten, maybe. Toff fellers. Planty toff. From the boat."

"I getcha. Told ya, Cap. Old Cartwright's wolf pack. But they don't savvy Mexico scrappin'. I got a longin' to lamp that yegg you sapped. You," he said, addressing the interpreter. "From now on, you're sergeant with double pay. If one of them *hombres* goes wrong, I'm killing you personal. Get the idea?"

"*Sí, señor.*"

"Want the job?"

"*¡Sí, sí!*"

"Then take charge of 'em. Herd 'em out there in the open an' keep 'em where I can keep a count on 'em. Come on, Cap."

A few moments later they were watching the slowly reviving white man, who they had propped into a sitting position, his back against a tree.

"Merry Christmas, Benny." Conomy grinned. "I thought you was still in the Big House."

"Pinch me fer a dip if it ain't Kid Conomy!" gasped the tin-eared, flat-nosed specimen. "Wot de hell's the big notion?"

Conomy turned to MacLane. "This gent is Sleigh Bells Benny. You seen the package I took off him? That's his snow, see . . . cocaine. He's all snowed under now, but it'll wear off after a while. When it does, he'll yap his head off. Double-cross his grandmother for a sniff of the white stuff. He's no good. Never was. Turned state's evidence when they sent him up. Bet a million Cartwright sprung him outta the can. But he'll crook his boss for a thin dime. I've knowed him fer ten years an' never yet knowed him to do anything that was halfway white. He's a damned rat, Cap. Do we croak him now or wait till after he's talked some?" Conomy was loading his Colts as he spoke.

"Dere ain't nothin' ta say, see?" Benny snarled a string of curses. "Lemme up an' I'll clean house wit' de two uh youse."

"Yeah? Cut 'im loose, Cap. I'll try him out."

"Let him up, Conomy?"

"Sure. I'm givin' him about fifteen pounds an' they say he usta be good. I wanna try him." Conomy handed Mac-Lane his gun and the package of cocaine. "If he licks me, give him his hop."

MacLane cut the ropes. Benny was on his feet, crouched and waiting, in the attitude of a fighter. Conomy spat out his tobacco and squared off.

"C'mon, ya louse!"

It was an odd fight, there on a Mexican mesa. Two heavyweights, both past masters at boxing and roughhouse fighting. They sparred for a moment or two, bobbing, side-stepping, feeling the other man out. The moonlight shed a pale white glow on the scene. The Mexicans stood at awed attention, watching the bout. MacLane stood apart, an interested spectator.

Then they mixed furiously. Swings, jabs, uppercuts, hooks. In and out, slashing, battering past guards, toe to toe sometimes. Clenching, breaking, tearing back into close fighting. Fists, sledgehammer fists spatted against bone and flesh. Blood spurted. The sound of their heavy breathing was punctured with grunts as they swapped punches.

Conomy tripped, dropped to one knee. Benny charged with a muttered curse, swinging at the kneeling man. Conomy ducked, his doubled body catapulting into the other's legs. Benny somersaulted and went over, his bulky form skidding across the flinty surface of the black lava mesa. Conomy pulled a sleeve across his battered face and laughed shortly.

"Stand up an' fight, rat!"

Benny, his face lacerated by the rough ground, was on his feet like a cat, advancing more cautiously. Conomy shot out a left, countered a wicked swing, and went in. A jab that seemed to travel but a scant foot caught Benny under the breastbone, lifted him, then dropped him in a moaning heap. Conomy stood back, breathing heavily.

"Got enough, rat?"

The agony of the solar plexus blow had

sickened the other man beyond speech. Still Conomy waited, fists knotted.

"He's got enough, Sarge."

"Yeah. An' he's gonna get more. He's a rat, a filthy, squealin' rat. I'm gonna kill him."

It was a whining, crawling, fawning Benny who some minutes later begged for his life. Conomy cuffed him and pushed him over with the heel of his hand.

"Stand up an' fight, ya yellow dog!"

"I'm licked, Kid! Ain't I tellin' ya I got plenty! Ya wouldn't croak me here, Kid! Gawd, Kid, don't!"

"Gonna talk?" snarled Conomy.

"Gawd, yes, Kid! Don't hit a guy! I'll squawk."

Sleigh Bells Benny talked, talked for the better part of half an hour, answering every question put to him. He was a whining, nerve-wracked wreck at the finish, begging for the drug that his body and nerves so craved. Pitiful, horrible, nauseating.

Conomy gave him the package and pointed to the trail.

"Hit the grit, Sleigh Bells. Go back an' tell Cartwright you squealed. Slide for the home base, rat."

"They'll kill me if I go back now!"

"I'll kill ya if ya stay," said Conomy

grimly. "Pick up your marbles an' go home. If you're scairt of Cartwright, hide out an' catch a fishin' boat outta San Quentin. Go back to Frisco an' your stinkin' hop joints. Stay there. Next time you get in my way, I'll gut-shoot ya. Git!"

When the man had gone down the trail, Conomy turned to MacLane.

"He was spillin' the truth, Cap. That's Cartwright's boat an' the old man's on it. They're playin' fer bigger stakes than that buried gold. Looks to me like there was a revolution about tuh bust this country wide open. Guns planted. That fast boat. Contact established with the interior. Enough tough *gringos* to keep up the morale uh the spics. We've dove into one sweet mess. Cartwright took San Quentin, or as good as took it. Cap, you got education an' brains. Got any ideas handy?"

"First," said MacLane promptly, "we'll get word to Pasqual and Atkins. Then you and I are going to work on that ship and we won't lay off till she's ready to hop off. Pick one of those Mexicans that looks halfway trustworthy and I'll send Atkins a message."

"Send him word ta go back?"

"Send him word to run, Sarge. He's badly out-numbered. Can't possibly win.

His best bet is to head for the nearest federal camp and tip them off to this game. Cartwright must be crazy."

"Not as loco as ya think, Cap. If he kin put in a big enough man, a gent with a big following here, the government will accept him rather than get into a scrap that'll cost a bunch uh dough. It's the guy with the backin' that sits pretty down here, regardless. At least, that's the way it looks to me. Once he puts it over with a rush, the game is his. Ports locked. Border patrolled. Me an' you an' Atkins an' Jones an' Pasqual will get our backs shoved against the 'dobe wall an' our fronts will be shot at by a bunch uh bad-shootin' Mexicans. You're right, Cap. Our best bet is to throw in with the government an' help squash this two-bit revolution. I'll go pick us a man to carry that note."

Preposterous as Cartwright's plan seemed, it was bold enough to stand a chance of success. Doubtless there were others besides Cartwright mixed up in it. Men of wealth and without scruples. Land pirates, men whose covetous eyes had long been fastened on the rich mines and grazing lands of harassed Mexico, whose government wobbled on unsteady legs. A land ripped and torn by revolutions and counter-revolutions; whose *peón* element fought in blind ignorance; whose faith had been betrayed time and again by mercenary leaders. Easily swayed by the oratory of men whose tongues were smooth and whose ambitions were sordid, these people of Mexico might again be led to bloody slaughter that a few Americans might gain wealth.

Cartwright and others, millions behind them, were eager to loot this land of vast wealth. To gain their ends, they would stoop to any sort of methods. Piracy, brigandage, murder. Their lust for gold and power had long since warped their reasoning of wrong and right.

MacLane knew this. He saw the wisdom of Conomy's prophesy. There was a chance of success for Cartwright. A desperate chance, but nevertheless a chance. With many millions at stake, it was a chance worth the taking.

What of Atkins and Pasqual and the others of this little band of adventurers? What chance had they of surviving? One chance in a million. Their backs against the wall, they must fight. Fight to the end. They had no recourse, no compromise. They were marked men. Outnumbered, surrounded, trapped.

It is at times like this that a man proves himself. Either he whines or he laughs. And now, as Stuart MacLane viewed the situation, he laughed.

Conomy, coming with a Mexican, stared at him, puzzled.

VIII

Now and then some man accomplishes the impossible and history is made. So it was with Conomy and Stuart MacLane that night in Mexico. The impossible task of assembling a plane with the aid of a few ignorant *peónes* was being accomplished. As for the history making — *quién sabe?*

A heartbreaking task. Dust and sweat and always the lurking danger of attack. And from the cañons surrounding the sinister Black Agate Mesa came desultory firing of guns. MacLane could but hope against hope that his message had reached Atkins.

Both he and Conomy knew what sacrifice they made in the sending of that message. It meant that their friends would move on as fast as possible. That two Americans and a handful of untrustworthy Mexicans were alone against a greater enemy. Yet neither the red-necked sergeant nor the grim-lipped MacLane voiced a word of complaint. Each did the work of five men. Straining, lifting, twisting turn-buckles until their fingers were raw and bleeding. Bolting in a motor that was un-wieldy, fastening on wings and landing gear, mounting the propeller and machine-gun. MacLane testing with expert care and swiftness each wire and strut. Conomy swearing lovingly as he fitted the gun to its carriage.

The sound of firing grew dimmer with each passing hour. The guard at the top of the trail sounded no alarm. After a time they heard no more shooting. Under the rim of the skyline showed the first gray line of a coming dawn. Conomy blocked the wheels and MacLane climbed into the cockpit. MacLane called the interpreter.

"Here's some money. About two hun-dred dollars . . . all I have. Take it and pay your men and yourself. God willing, you can go back home and fight no more. You and the others are brave men. I salute you, *señor*." He saluted the impressed Mexican and leaned his head over the side. "Prime 'er, Sarge."

"Off." Conomy was asking for a dead motor.

"Off," repeated MacLane, making sure the switch was off. Conomy pulled the propeller over on compression, blade parallel with the ground.

Thus to crank a small plane is a common enough job. Always dangerous, but to the practiced mechanic or pilot, all in a day's work. Yet this big motor was different. Ordinarily, when cranking a DeHaviland, three men joined hands and the instant the man grasping the propeller pulled the blade toward him, the other two men jerked him away. But MacLane had seen big Conomy crank more than one DeHaviland alone, while men of lesser build looked on in awed admiration.

Conomy stepped a little to one side and rubbed the palm of his big hands on his breeches. He grinned up at MacLane.

"Contact!" he called.

"Contact!" returned MacLane, and slipped on the switch. Conomy, hands grasping the prop blade, swung his right leg upward, gave the blade a swift pull, and, spinning about, threw himself clear. With a belching cough, a kick back, and a roar, the motor thundered in the still, gray light. Fate, in a generous moment, had surpassed their wildest hopes and given life to a motor that, ninety-nine times out of a 100, would have failed to respond so quickly.

MacLane throttled the motor to the proper number of revolutions for the warming process and grinned at Conomy who was doing a good imitation of an Indian war dance. Suddenly the dancer paused, staring toward the head of the trail. Across that strip of black tableland came a score of racing horsemen, shooting as they came. Conomy jerked the blocks free and clambered into the rear cockpit, fastening his safety belt with deft hands. MacLane nodded and slowly opened the throttle. The big plane moved forward, gained speed. MacLane pulled his stick back and leveled the tail upward. Then, with a muttered prayer, he gave her the gun.

They took the air staggering.

A cold motor that was going on its maiden flight without the preliminary ten-block examination. A rough country where landing meant a wreck and almost certain death. But that was the chance they took.

Bullets whined like a drove of hornets. Conomy, his cheek filled with plug tobacco, merely grinned down at the rushing attackers and waved a derisive farewell, albeit his heart was pounding like a trip hammer and his ears were listening to the steady roar of the motor.

Flame sprayed from the exhaust pipes, eerie in the fading darkness of the passing night. The ship tipped upward into a purple sky sprinkled with pale stars. Climbing, roaring, unfaltering in its ascent. Conomy saw the background recede from under them. MacLane, hands steady, neck rigid, steel-nerved, might have been testing out a ship from a training field, so nonchalant was his attitude. Yet, inside, he was tingling with excitement and fear. But his airman's thrill of the feel of a ship held him in its spell. Again he was Captain Stuart MacLane of the U.S. Air Corps.

The air whipped their unhelmeted heads and tears streamed from ungoggled eyes unused to the terrific speed. MacLane, grinning into the wind, kept climbing until their altitude was sufficient to pass over the black peaks ahead. Then, Atkins's map strapped on one knee where he could readily study it without inconvenience, he took his compass readings and headed for a spot on the map marked **Casitas**. It was an inland town, federal outpost of the Mexican army. 100 miles, air line, and, if the somewhat inadequate topography of the map could be trusted, Casitas lay in a level country that might afford some sort of landing field.

He and Conomy, in their Army days, had established a code of communication while in the air where the roar of a motor made speech impossible. The code was the one-hand deaf and dumb alphabet. He now held up one hand and swiftly spelled out his intentions. Conomy nodded when MacLane turned his head questioningly.

"Atta pilot," Conomy replied in the code, and spat over the side of the rushing ship. The big sergeant, as became his position as observer, divided his attention between the air and the ground. Presently he signaled MacLane and pointed downward.

It was daylight now, and the first streaks of a rising sun showed dead ahead on the broken skyline. They were flying over a comparatively level country, and far below them a series of black dots, like a string of black ants, crawled along a trail that wound through the mesquite and catclaw.

MacLane nodded and swung groundward in long, slow spirals. Then he shoved his stick forward and they shot downward at a steep glide. A scant 100 feet above the halted column, he leveled off.

There was Atkins and Pasqual. Jones, on his mule. The soldiers. MacLane could almost see the looks of startled wonderment on their faces. Atkins was waving his hat.

There was no place to land. MacLane signaled to Conomy: "Wigwag Atkins our destination." He swung upward, banked, and again flew over the halted column. Conomy's arms moved in the semaphore message. Pasqual was answering.

"OK," came the ground. "OK. Close followed. Desperate. Bring troops. Revolution on. Stand at Diablo Lake."

MacLane waved, then was off. Diablo Lake. He found it on his map.

"Fort at Diablo Lake," Conomy signaled. "Deserted. Got a hunch gold buried there."

They had climbed to a safe flying altitude now and could converse while the big plane carried them onward at terrific speed.

"What do you mean . . . gold at Diablo Lake?" signaled MacLane.

"Pasqual not so good. Lied to Atkins about location," came the startling reply.

"What's the idea?"

"Damned if I know," signaled Conomy. "Jones told me. Jones is wise. Remember Pasqual has a last name and it's Goldberg."

MacLane nodded, a little sick at heart. He rather liked Pasqual in a way, although the half-caste was not a type to be implicitly trusted. Atkins had vouched for him. Pasqual owed his very life to Atkins. Then why had Pasqual lied about the location of the gold?

"You sure Jones was right?" he signaled.

"Sure."

"Why so sure?"

"Because," came Conomy's answer, "Jones helped bury it there."

This was a new complication. MacLane scowled at his instrument board, trying to puzzle it all out. He hated to think of Pasqual as a traitor. But if he was, what then? What was his attitude toward the others in the party? And why had Pasqual, knowing that Atkins was giving MacLane the wrong instructions regarding the location of the gold, allowed him to do so? What would have happened if MacLane were to have landed at Sierra Blanca and Poison Wells?

Still trying to untangle the mental snarl in his brain, MacLane drove his ship with his wide-open throttle, eyes watching his compass needle.

Conomy signaled. There was something of startled importance in the swift movement of the observer's fingered wording.

"Look back. Left. Up. Plane coming."

MacLane looked, but his wind-whipped eyes saw nothing. Conomy pointed. Then the grim-jawed pilot made out a black spot against the cloudless sky.

That would be Lee Cartwright. Cartwright and Cline in the scout plane. Seeing what they could see. No doubt directing the movements of the enemy cavalry. Perhaps searching the sky for the bomber, if news of Atkins's De Haviland in its crate on the mesa had reached enemy ears.

Then a cluster of drab adobe buildings showed on the ground below, not two miles distant. Green trees showed like patches of green rugs laid on a yellow floor. MacLane pointed and Conomy grinned. That would be Casitas, the federal outpost.

They could see people quit their houses and rush into the street, faces lifted skyward, gaping at the unaccustomed sight of an airplane. Perhaps most of them had never seen a plane. MacLane circled the town, hunting a landing spot. Lower and lower, motor idling. In front of the *cuartel,* troops were pouring into formation. Like ants discovering some danger threatening their home. Lower. MacLane picked a spot that looked like it might be a parade ground or drill field. He glided, landed with the light grace of a huge bird, sped over the level adobe ground, and taxied back the length of the field toward the gaping mob of Mexican soldiers and towns-people. He cut his motor and climbed out of the cockpit to face a line of leveled rifles and a flustered little officer in ill-fitting khaki.

MacLane halted. Recalling the military manner of Tommy Atkins, he clicked his boot heels and stiffly saluted.

"Por Dios, señor," barked the officer, "who are you and what is the reason of this visit?" He spoke good English, and, despite his badly fitting garb, there was a trim military air about him.

"You are in command here, sir?" asked MacLane, suppressing a desire to grin.

"I have that doubtful honor."

"Then I have a message for you of grave importance. There is a rebel movement on its way. We come to warn you."

"Why?" The officer's voice was cold with suspicion. It was altogether unusual for a *gringo* to side with the government and the officer plainly scented a trap.

"Because the lives of friends are at stake, sir. They are even now running from this rebel army that comes from San Quentin."

"Aha!" The officer smiled nastily. "And it will be that thrice-cursed meddler of a Pasqual Goldberg leading them, eh? From

his San Quentin. Quite so, *señor.* Quite probable."

"But quite the opposite," replied Mac-Lane, smiling.

"Eh? What's that?"

"It is Pasqual Goldberg who they are chasing, sir."

"Then his own pack of jackals have turned on their leader?"

"Not at all. A man named Cartwright heads the rebel movement."

"This is no time or place for crude joking, *Señor Americano,*" said the officer, scowling. "*Señor* Cartwright is a staunch friend of the government of Mexico. Pasqual Goldberg is the worst agitator we have. Perhaps you have been drinking, *señor?*" There was a cutting insolence to the Mexican's tone that made the American long to slap him. But he held his temper.

"I am neither joking nor am I drunk, *señor.* Quite the contrary. I am Captain Stuart MacLane of the United States Army. My companion is Sergeant Conomy of the same outfit. We came to warn you. Even now Cartwright blocks the port of San Quentin with an armed sub-chaser flying false colors. His army, made up of desperate criminals and near criminals from the United States, is coming this way by forced marches. Among his black-leg American fighters is a sprinkling of Mexicans in the federal uniform. Deserters, no doubt, from the little San Quentin garrison. I give you this information as a gentleman and an officer of the United States Army."

"And in that case," said the Mexican officer crisply, "you are violating the international laws of neutrality by flying an armed plane into Mexico. Can you explain that away, *Señor* Captain?" The man's tone was insulting now. Conomy, in the gun pit, stirred uneasily.

MacLane faced the officer and the line of leveled rifles. The situation was a bad one.

"My plane is privately owned," he said stiffly. "I am here in Mexico unofficially. As a matter of fact, I am no longer an officer in the United States Army."

"And in that case," came the sneering reply, "will you please state the nature of the business that brings two Americans into this part of Mexico in an armed plane? Both of you are liable to arrest for violation of the embargo on arms into this country. It would seem, Captain MacLane, that you have a great deal to explain."

Conomy had crawled from his gun pit and was fooling about the ship. He had leaned across the pilot's cockpit muttering in a plainly audible voice something about a leak in the gas line. But as he passed MacLane, he had whispered in a barely audible undertone: "Booster. Hop 'er when I mote."

The plane was equipped with a booster that will sometimes start a warm motor. Conomy meant to start the plane and MacLane was to hop it as the nervy sergeant spun the ship about and took off.

"Your attitude is most discourteous." MacLane, facing the officer and the line of rifles, spoke with military crispness. "We come with a message of warning and you treat us as criminals. In which case, *señor,* we'll be going." In a flash, MacLane's six-shooter was out, covering the astonished officer. His words rasped: "One word to those lousy, misfit 'dobe tin soldiers and I'll drill you. Get that? Tell them to lower their guns."

"So?" The little officer stiffened like some bantam rooster. "*Señor,* you cannot put over the Yankee bluff on Captain Hermano Ortega. I here place you both under arrest. Men, attention. Should the *gringos* make the attempt to escape, shoot to kill them. Now, *Señor Gringo,* shoot me and be damned. For you will be dead before I hit the ground."

"Set, Sarge?" gritted MacLane, lips tightening.

"Yo." There was a little whir of the booster. Then the huge motor roared. Dust and sand filled the air as the ship skidded around. MacLane was hidden in the dust. The Mexican officer and his men were blinded by the miniature hurricane of dust and sand. MacLane, with a swift leap, grabbed the edge of the rear cockpit as Conomy taxied across the ground, tail toward the soldiers, who had now commenced shooting. The ship's tail came up, the big craft took on speed. To the two men, it seemed years. Eternity. Bullets spatted about them, ripping holes in fuselage and wings. MacLane climbed over into the front cockpit and took the stick from the grinning Conomy, who stepped out on the wing and back into the gunner's pit.

Dust, a roaring, fire-belching motor. Then up, up, toward the blessed blue of safety above them. Conomy, back in his cockpit, thumbed his nose at the frantic officer, who was emptying two Lugers at them in furious anger.

MacLane was torn between bitter anger and a queer sort of mirth. Not until they had climbed to a thousand feet and into the safety zone did he realize the grave danger they had just escaped. A shiver ran down his spine as he recalled the line of the muzzles, each gun seemingly pointed squarely at him. Angry as he was, he could not help but admire the game-cock courage of that little officer in his misfit khaki.

He glanced at his map, took his bearings, and steered for Diablo Lake. He felt rather bewildered as to what course he should pursue. No aid was to be gotten from the federal troops at Casitas. Atkins and the others were crowding for the meager refuge of some abandoned fort at this lake, pursued by a large force of fighting men who would give no quarter.

He signaled Conomy: "Any suggestions?"

"Go get Cartwright and Cline," came the prompt reply. Conomy bit off a fresh corner of plug and patted his Lewis gun as MacLane turned his head. Then the big sergeant pointed upward into the blue sky where a black dot showed.

MacLane nodded and sent back a message: "Do not shoot. I am going to drive

100

him down to the ground."

Conomy swore lustily and lengthily, but his words were obliterated by the roar of the big motor. MacLane was climbing upward, heading for the black speck in the sky that was Lee Cartwright in his fast scout plane. Flirting with suicide, from the standpoint of Conomy. Superior flyer as he was, it would be a well-nigh impossible feat to lick Cartwright and force him down without shooting him down. They had no parachutes. They were after a plane that could fly circles around them. And Cline would be peppering them with machine-gun fire. Suicide, nothing less. Yet Conomy only grinned through set teeth and signaled: "Hop to it, you damned fool."

IX

Captain MacLane had been Lee Cartwright's instructor in acrobatic flying. Between instructor and pupil lay buried a secret. To Cartwright, it was a secret of shame and he hated MacLane the more bitterly for it. That secret was this: Lee Cartwright had voluntarily quit combat flying after his first solo flight at that hair-raising, dangerous game. Sobbing, shaking with the terror of half an hour in the air with MacLane in another ship waging mock battle, he had blurted that fear into the sun-baked ears of the wild-flying MacLane.

"I can't do it, Mac! By God, I won't! Not for you or any other man. It's murder, turning a man loose with so little dual work! Murder, damn you! They can bust me, do what they damn' please, I tell you! I won't go up again. It's murder!"

Now, as MacLane climbed up toward the scout plane that hung in the sky like a buzzard seeking its carrion, he recalled that day of Cartwright's dismissal. The look of bitter, jealous hatred in the man's eyes, the muttered threat as the disgraced flyer walked away. It was while Cartwright was waiting transfer to bombing school that MacLane had been court-martialed.

MacLane now knew that it was Cartwright and Cline who had planned and successfully carried out his disgrace despite his splendid record. Barracks rumor had it that MacLane had fired Cartwright from pursuit school out of petty jealousy. It had its believers, and, as is the way of black rumor, it had not reached the ears of MacLane or Conomy. Now MacLane, in a heavy, cumbersome ship, was climbing up to meet the man who had broken him and perhaps wrecked his life. Above him droned the big ship and its two passengers.

MacLane, the superior flyer, relied on his ability to keep out of the line of Cline's fire. Mostly, however, he was betting on the psychological angle of it — Cartwright's mental funk when he saw the man he so hated, the man who knew the yellow taint in his heart, up in the air with him. Cartwright had no way of knowing who piloted the D.H. His very attitude now as he soared in easy circles was one of curiosity, rather than enmity. Perhaps he thought it a friendly ship belonging to his father's expedition. At any rate, the pilot of the scout plane was showing neither alarm nor animosity. Then Cartwright, as if to impress the pilot of the heavier ship, shoved the nose of his ship into a spin and dropped down out of the sky.

MacLane pulled his stick back a little, climbing, eyes on the spinning ship that now dropped below him and leveled off with a scream of straining struts.

"The damn' fool!" grunted MacLane, and, whipping the big nose of the D.H. over and down, dove for the smaller plane that was banking for a turn. "Showing off, eh? Thinks I belong to his outfit." He leveled off and flew squarely at the scout ship, fully at the ship, without a motion of swerving, throttle wide open. Conomy set his jaws and waited for the crash. But Cartwright, in white-lipped terror, dove underneath the other ship that had apparently tried to ram him.

MacLane banked, then side-slipped. Leveling with a moaning screech, he came at the scout again, then turned, skidding the turn and passing the scout so closely that Cartwright instinctively dived. But MacLane knew that, before he dived, Cartwright had recognized the pilot of the big D.H. He had seen Cartwright's jaw drop with astonishment. He had seen Cline turn to look. Conomy, standing upright in his cockpit, had made significant motions with his gun.

Now began as peculiar an air battle as was ever waged. Fear-driven as he was, Cartwright was attempting to shoot down the bigger ship. He climbed now, out of reach of the slower ship. Up, up, Cline manning one gun. The second gun, mounted on the front cowl and synchronized to shoot through the prop, was worked by the trigger mechanism on the pilot's stick.

They were over the D.H. now, momentarily hidden from MacLane by the big ship's blind spot. Then they shot into view, diving down, pilot's gun spitting flame. Lancing bullets whined and smoking tracer slashed. *Rat-tat-tat-tat!*

MacLane side-slipped out of the way, and, as Cline's gun rattled, dived squarely at the scout that Cartwright's inferior brand of flying had let drop too low. Cartwright, face set and white under the goggles, tried to dodge, but MacLane followed him. Straight at the little ship again. It seemed to Conomy that the wings lapped as they shot past. That luck alone had saved both planes from going down in a splintered mass. Yet the big sergeant knew that it was the skilful hand of MacLane that had piloted them clear. In spite of the tingling sensation along his spine, Conomy felt secure.

"I'll be white-headed when we land," he growled, thumbing his nose at the tight-jawed Cline, whose gun had jammed.

MacLane shot a swift glance at his altimeter. They had dropped 2,000 feet. Again the little ship was below. MacLane looped over without cutting his motor. A roaring loop of hell that came once more straight at the ship that was maneuvering in crazy panic. They missed the scout's tail by mere inches, it seemed. But they came away with a riddled fuselage. For the desperate Cline had poured a burst from his corrected gun. Conomy chewed and spat.

"Whew!" he grunted. "Damn near made a hit. Next time, orders or no orders, I turn my rattler loose, you polecat."

But that next time was not to come. As MacLane swung his ship about, both he and Conomy saw that which sent a sickening lump into their throats. For it was murder, or attempted murder, that they witnessed. The act of a craven. A deed that sank lower than mere cowardice. That was the thing they saw from above.

For Lee Cartwright had left his cockpit

and had jumped, trusting to the parachute strapped to his shoulders. And Cline, for some unaccountable reason, was not equipped with a parachute. Moreover, Cline was in the rear cockpit, from which the stick had been removed. Alone in a ship that was going down without a pilot, spinning now toward the ground below.

They saw Cartwright's parachute open, then float lazily down with its burden. They saw Cline slip his safety belt and commence crawling for the front cockpit to reach the control stick. He had gained the edge of the front cockpit when the horrible, sickening crash came. What had been a graceful air machine was now a mass of twisted steel and shattered wood. And in that wreckage lay Cline. Murdered, if ever a man was murdered.

MacLane headed for the parachute. He felt sick inside, shaken by what he had seen. For a moment he felt the red rage of a killer and pointed the ship squarely at the man who was floating down to a safe landing. Then, when almost upon the helpless, white-faced Cartwright, who thought death was crashing at him, MacLane zoomed. Conomy hurled a profane taunt at the panicky man as they passed. Then, soaring in wide circles, they followed Cartwright down out of a windless sky to the sandy waste of a desert below. They had landed before the parachute dropped its cowardly burden to safety. But as they ran toward the wilted parachute, they saw Cartwright jerk his gun.

"Get back, damn you!" screamed the man whose nerves were wholly gone. His automatic spattered bullets whistling past MacLane's head. But MacLane, running toward the man as swiftly as the heavy sand permitted, did not slacken pace. As the automatic snapped empty, MacLane was on him.

All the pent-up bitterness in MacLane's heart now loosened and swept up into his brain, distorting it. He was, for the moment, insane with the lust to kill this human thing that had so hurt him, this craven-souled, murdering jackal that had deserted a comrade and sent him to destruction. And when Conomy sought to pull him off the screaming, moaning Cartwright, he fought Conomy with a fury that required all the ex-sergeant's bull strength to defeat. Only when Conomy sat on him and held him for long moments did that red rage die. He was sobbing horribly when Conomy slid off him and threw a gorilla-like arm across his shoulders.

"You got 'im, Skipper. You smeared 'im plenty. Man, you sure ruined that sweet map uh his. Lookit his nose. Pipe them shiners he's gonna have. I'll tie him up while he's sleepin'. Then let's take a squint at Cline." He pulled a plug of tobacco from somewhere. "Chaw, Skipper? No? Then roll a smoke while I'm hog-tyin' this yella dog."

But MacLane was too shaky to roll a cigarette and it was the red-faced, perspiring Conomy who constructed the smoke, then lit it. Then they traversed the quarter mile of heavy sand and found Cline. A broken, moaning mass of bloody flesh and bone, but still living and conscious.

"My trail's ended." Cline looked at them with pain-seared eyes. "All smashed to hell. Cartwright . . . quit me. You seen him, Captain?"

"All of it, old man."

"I'm croakin'. Croakin', Captain. Cartwright landed safe?"

"Yes."

"I'd like to take him ta hell with me. If ya'd carry me where he is an' gimme a gun, I'd take him along where I'm goin'."

"Sorry, Cline, but we can't stand for that even if it's what he has coming."

"It was him that crooked you, MacLane.

I'll swear it. Lemme at 'im."

"Sign what I put on paper," said MacLane grimly, "and I'll do the getting." He took out a fountain pen and a notebook. "Who put the whiskey in my ship that morning, Cline?"

"Me. Cartwright paid me, see. Him an' me filed the control wires to where they'd still get by ordinary inspection, but when you put strain on 'em, they'd snap. I got paid good. Cartwright swiped the squadron funds and give 'em to me for pay. Lemme croak him, MacLane."

"Sign this, instead. If we get Cartwright out of Mexico, he'll do life in the federal prison. That'll be worse than death for him."

"Not so bad." Cline made a grimace that was meant for a grin. He signed the paper and lay back, his eyes filming with the approach of death. Conomy put a cigarette between the dying man's lips.

"Thanks, Conomy. More'n I deserve." And so he died. MacLane covered the dead man's face with the torn, leather flying coat. Then they trudged back to where they had left Cartwright.

X

Diablo Lake lay like a mammoth sapphire in an emerald setting. An oasis in the middle of arid desolation. In the ruins of a granite-walled fortress, a handful of weary men fought for their lives against horrible odds.

Throughout an endless morning and into a sun-blistered, sweltering afternoon, they counted their shots and watched for the coming of the federal troops. But no troops came. The hail of hot lead splattered against the walls. Men died, whimpering or praying or cursing, according to their breed. Atkins's left arm was in a blood-smeared sling. A Mauser bullet had ripped open the cheek of Pig Iron Jones. Pasqual Goldberg, unhurt, ran the gauntlet of fire time and again, fetching back skin water sacks from the lake that lay twenty yards from the fort. A few complained, but mostly they fought with silent grimness. And their rifles were taking toll of enemy lives. The enemy, who lay in hastily dug trenches or behind rocks and brush.

Atkins knew, and Jones and Pasqual Goldberg knew, that with the coming of night their fate was sealed. Under the cloak of darkness, the enemy would swarm into the ruined fort and by sheer numbers wipe them out.

"It won't be long now," Jones muttered in an undertone. "Ammunition gettin' low. But I'm takin' a few with me before I go out."

Then out of the sky came the distant drone of a high-powered motor. A speck took shape. Became an airplane. A cheer went up from the besieged men inside the rock walls. The ship circled. Two heads peered down, and arms waved greeting. Then the ship circled lower and the heads disappeared.

Now it banked, throttle wide open, a scant ten feet, it seemed, above the heads of the entrenched men. And Kid Conomy, standing with braced legs, held in by his safety belt, raked that trench with a rattling machine-gun fire as MacLane tore on with open throttle.

Again they came, and again. Six times in all. Then they took altitude while the to-bacco-chewing Conomy loaded the six empty magazines. Wounded men groaned and cursed in the trenches. They had wasted good lead shooting at that speeding ship and its grinning gunner.

Now it came down at them again out of the sky. Roaring, cracking, and Conomy's gun spitting death at them. Panic seized them now and they ran, deaf to the cursing orders of their leaders. The ship zoomed, banked, side-slipped down, and leveled off. Conomy slapped on a fresh magazine and sprayed two men who seemed to be leaders. They started to run, stumbled, went down, and then lay still.

"Up and at 'em, boys!" yelled Atkins.

"Give 'em the gaff!" bawled Jones.

Pasqual barked crisp orders, and the three led their yelling, victory-drunk followers in a wild charge that swept the enemy before them. MacLane, flying low — "cutting grass" as Conomy put it — chased the bunches of men who sought to make a stand. Scattering them like quail.

Then the motor sputtered, cut out, and went dead. The big ship, too low to level off for a dead-stick landing, slid down on one wing, crumpled in a rending, splintering heap, and two bruised and shaken men unsnapped their safety belts and scrambled out. MacLane's nose was bleeding and his lips were split. Conomy doubled up, coughing and gagging.

"God!" MacLane saw blood gushing from Conomy's mouth. "They hit you, Sarge?"

Conomy spit blood mixed with brown tobacco juice, pulled a sleeve across his mouth, then, reaching into the bloody cavity, drew forth two teeth. Again he spit, then grinned ruefully.

"Paid thirty bucks in Hoboken fer them molars," he grunted. "That tooth carpenter claimed they was punch-proof. He lied, damn 'im. Swallered a fresh chaw when we hit. But, by God, Mac, we won the war!"

He was back up in the cockpit, hauling at some inert bulk. He dragged a bound and badly frightened Lee Cartwright out onto the sand.

"I was hopin' you was dead," he grunted, then once more crawled into the plane and emerged with a triumphant grin, gingerly carrying something wrapped in a leather coat.

Carefully he unwrapped the coat, then held aloft a quart bottle filled with colorless liquid.

"A little soothin' syrup, Skipper. Held out on Pig Iron. Tequila. And this time,

Cartwright, you yellow-hearted hound pup, it wasn't planted in our ship, neither. Join me, Cap? No? Well, here's bad 'cess to that tooth carpenter. This bottle neck fits into the hole they left in my lower jaw."

Apparently they had the little open stretch of sand to themselves, but not so the next moment. A running squad of men came out of the brush. MacLane reached for his gun, then recognized Jones among them.

"Come on, you sea dog!" bawled Conomy. "Run, you bowlegged walrus, or I'll drink 'er all."

MacLane waved a welcome to Atkins and Pasqual, who now emerged from the other side of the brush thicket, followed by sweating, ragged soldiers.

" 'Jove, Mac, old boy," he croaked huskily as he wrung MacLane's hand. "You saved us, old chap. I say, I . . . I . . . gad, man, we. . . ."

"Apple sauce!" MacLane, red with embarrassment, grinned foolishly.

Pasqual came up, halted, and, clicking his heels, saluted. "Ees not so damn' frequent, *señor,* that one salutes so brave a man. Me, I cannot shake the 'and until I tell you something. After I 'ave tol' you,

you shall take my gun an' shoot me an' I shall die, *señor*."

Atkins smiled.

"He refers, Mac, to the gold. Seems the stuff is here, not at Sierra Blanca. There was to be some lead sewed up in canvas at Sierra Blanca. That was to be your cargo. There would be men to load it, then you would land it at San Quentin onto a boat that would be followed, because information of your flight would reach San Quentin shortly after the supposed gold was loaded on the boat. Meanwhile, the real stuff was to go over by mule train to a hidden bay where Jones would be waiting.

"You were to be well paid, and your danger in the escapade was not great. But poor, loyal Pasqual, because he thinks he owes his life to me and fancies I'm badly in need of a large sum of money, wished to give me the lion's share. He told me about it today. Saw the fallacy of his plans and all that. Acted according to his lights and felt all cut up when I acted muffled about his lying."

Pasqual bowed stiffly, his face set in stern lines. "I 'ave lie to my frien's. I 'ave done w'at I never 'ave done before. That double-cross. Here ees my gon, *señor*. Shoot."

MacLane took the gun, then handed it back, butt first, and gripped the hand of Pasqual Goldberg, who would violate his code of honor in the name of loyalty and friendship.

Conomy passed his bottle, and then it was a light-hearted crowd that plodded across the sand to the fort.

But that joy was short-lived. MacLane, with Atkins's glasses, had picked up an approaching dust cloud that came from the direction of Casitas. Briefly he explained the unsuccessful plan for aid there, and the hostile attitude of the Mexican officer.

"*Caramba,* I was afraid for that," said Pasqual sadly. "That Ortega ees bad enemy for me. Ees too bad. We cannot run no more. The ammunition ees low."

"And the damn' pack of you," croaked Lee Cartwright, who Conomy had dumped against the wall in a sitting posture, "will decorate a wall with a firing squad in front of you. Ortega's a friend of mine and I'll have plenty to tell him."

"Yeah?" gritted Conomy, leaning over him. "Say the word, Cap, and I'll put this guy where he won't talk."

"No, let the whelp alone, Sarge. We're in Dutch anyhow and who knows, perhaps he's lying about knowing Ortega. If he is, he goes to the wall with us. We don't any of us know him except that his name is Smith and he's gone a little loco from the heat. Thinks he's Lee Cartwright. You might frisk him, Sarge, and remove all evidence of his identity."

Conomy searched him but found nothing of importance. MacLane puffed a cigarette and grinned.

"I hope, *Smith,* that you won't disgrace your race and your country by dying yellow. The least you can do to wipe out your craven past is to die like a man. Think it over, *Smith*."

It took the Mexican cavalry an hour to reach the fort. They were halted by a crisp challenge from Atkins.

"Your assistance is a bit tardy, Lieutenant. I. . . ."

"Assistance?" The little officer fairly barked the word. "Assistance, eh? I came, *señor,* to arrest you. You and Pasqual Goldberg and two *gringos* who fly an airplane. Will you surrender peacefully or shall I be forced to attack? In the latter case, I cannot be responsible for your safety or your lives. My men shoot well."

"Then they bin practicin' a hell of a lot

the past few hours," came the audible voice of Conomy.

"Supposing we surrender," put in Atkins, "what then?"

"You will be given the ordinary military trial."

"Trial by escape, perhaps?" Atkins referred to the *ley del fuego,* the murderous trial by fire whereby the prisoner is killed while attempting to escape. The officer seemed about to choke with emotion. Drawing himself to an even more erect position in his saddle, he twisted at a miniature, waxed mustache.

"I am Captain Hermano Ortega," he snapped. "I am an officer and a gentleman of honor by birth, not by the act of Yankee Congress. I do not lie, even to an enemy. When I give my word, I keep it. Your trial shall be unbiased."

"Where will this trial be held?"

"At Casitas, naturally."

"In that case, *Señor* Captain, we fight. Speaking for myself and my comrades, I demand that we be tried at San Carlos."

San Carlos was the military and civil headquarters of the lower part of the state. A thriving little seaport with a goodly sprinkling of Americans and English, Germans and French. Army base of the federals and the first port of call below San Quentin.

For a long moment, Ortega was silent, weighing the request. He was well fed up with the isolation of Casitas. Perhaps, if he brought in these prisoners and proof of smashing a revolution, he would be given a more pleasant post of command. Then, there would be no little pleasure in parading down the street with these prisoners. The envy of brother officers, the target of soft-eyed glances as he rode past *señoritas* in *mantillas* in the plaza.

" *'Sta bueno, señor.* It shall be San Carlos."

Atkins turned to Pasqual. So far none of the men in the fort had shown themselves. Atkins had remained out of sight as he talked.

"Can we trust this fellow's word, Pasqual?"

"Perfectly." Pasqual mounted the wall and threw Ortega an airy salute.

"*Buenos días,* Hermano. So they 'ave made you captain, eh? That ees good. *Santa María,* my frien', you get more littler each time I see you. Always, you 'ave been the small rooster. The gamecock, no? Per'aps, when you march into San Carlos weeth so many prisoner for the firing

120

squad, they make you major, no? Then you well afford the uniform that fits, eh? *Santa María,* Hermano, 'e must 'ave been the beeg man who die an' you take from heem that uniform, eh?" Pasqual chuckled, and, as Ortega sputtered incoherently, the half-caste turned to his friends: "We go to the military college together, Hermano an' me. Ees damn' smart, that Hermano Ortego. So hees father, who ees w'at you call the beeg cheese een Mexico City, send Hermano to the American college een California. Ees one damn' fine gentleman, that father of Hermano."

They filed out from the ruined fort and stacked arms at the feet of Ortega.

Again MacLane felt an odd desire to grin. The ragged, misfit army, the pomp and tin-soldier formality. Ortega rigid as a ramrod. His men at attention. The Mexican flag, hanging limply in the dead air, the color guard of Ortega's cavalry unshaven and pigmy-size under their enormous hats.

Pasqual's ragged, dust-coated men, faces stamped with stolid dejection, laid down their arms under the command of General Conomy. Atkins, Pasqual, and Conomy at attention. Jones was shifting uneasily on his seaman's legs. A burlesque surrender.

Yet tragic in its very comedy. For these men, leaders and privates, faced stark death.

"There are dead to be buried, Captain," spoke Atkins, when all stood unarmed. "Wounded to care for. Our men and those who fought us."

"That shall be taken care of. I leave a detail here for the purpose. A doctor and medical staff. I shall send back wagons for the wounded."

"And there is one of our men inside the fort, Captain, who has a touch of the sun. Quite balmy, poor chap. Fancies he's someone else. Yesterday, he was General Pershing, the day before he was the Pope. Now he fancies he is Lee Cartwright. Says he is your friend."

"I know no Lee Cartwright. There is a Cartwright, but he is elderly and dignified, and very rich. A friend of Mexico. He has a son named Lee Cartwright, but the son is not in Mexico."

"Surely." Atkins smiled. "This poor fellow has perhaps read too much. The sun has affected his mind. We were forced to tie him up, else he would have killed someone."

"He shall be taken care of." Ortega sent a squad in after the now sullen and badly frightened Lee Cartwright, who had heard Atkins's words.

So far, Ortega had ignored both Conomy and MacLane save for the hotly contemptuous glances he occasionally shot them. Conomy grinned at him and winked broadly at the Mexican soldiers, who returned the wink with a scowl.

Presently they were under way, the prisoners riding single file under heavy guard. Atkins, MacLane, and Pasqual were under extra heavy guard and so placed that communication was impossible.

Pasqual attempted to bribe Ortega but met with an insulting refusal.

"*Sí*, Hermano. Ees like I expec'. Like your father, you are too damn' hones'. Otherwise, my frien', you would be a general by now."

"And if you and your *amigos* were more honest," came the hot reply, "you would not be facing a firing squad at San Carlos."

XI

Captain Ortega made the most of his entry into the town of San Carlos. It was the hour when, *siestas* over, San Carlos strolled about the plaza listening to the band playing in its bandstand in the center of the plaza. Excitement ran like wildfire over the little Mexican town. They were there, *en masse,* to watch the prisoners being herded into the *cuartel.*

The common soldiers were left in the quadrangle or bullpen. The Americans, Atkins, and Pasqual were given a large room and a heavy guard stood at the door. Then they were left alone. From outside the *cuartel* came the shouting *vivas* of the populace, greeting Captain Ortega, hero of the day.

Among the prisoners in the huge cell was Lee Cartwright. MacLane undid his bonds and grinned down at him.

"Before we all get shot, Lee," he said easily, "it might be well for you to unburden your soul a little. Conomy and I saw what you did to Cline. Cline lived long enough to sign a confession that clears up our little Army deal."

"Yeah?" sneered Cartwright. "What of it? You'll never get out of Mexico to use that confession. Cline was a rat that needed poisoning. What are you going to do about it, MacLane?"

"That depends." MacLane smiled. "There is another little matter that is going to be cleared up, while we're on the subject of rats. How about that little ride you and Cline took one night in San Francisco? Campbell, your father's former partner, went along. He never came back from that ride. Cline swore he drove the car and you killed Campbell."

"He lied!" Cartwright had gone white as chalk. "He lied!"

"No, he didn't. Dying men don't lie." MacLane's tone hardened. "Lee Cartwright, I want the absolute truth out of you. Come clean, or I'll kill you now with my two hands! Out with it!" He shook Cartwright like a terrier shaking a rat.

"Kill 'em, Cap," urged Conomy.

MacLane flung the man roughly into a corner and stood back, eying him. "I'm waiting, Cartwright."

"Cline lied. I drove the car. Cline killed him."

"Who paid Cline? You?"

"Yes. But the money was my father's money. He's the guilty one. I was just a go-between. They can't hang me for that. They can't!"

His voice was a shrill screech. The guard looked through the bars of the door. Pasqual sputtered a few words in Spanish. The guard grinned and walked down the corridor.

"Put that in writing, Cartwright. God, you're lower than I thought. Squealing on your own father."

"He got me into this. He'll have to get me out."

"Here." MacLane handed him pen and paper. "Write as I dictate."

Lee Cartwright obeyed in whimpering silence. MacLane read the paper and put it in his wallet along with Cline's confession.

A guard brought supper, consisting of tough meat, beans, and tortillas. Later, another guard brought straw for bedding.

"I say," said Atkins, "is there any way of getting a note to the British consul down the street?"

"Per'aps." Pasqual took off a boot and, ripping a seam, pulled forth several United States banknotes of large denomination. "Write the note, *Señor* Atkins."

Pasqual went to the door and talked in a

low tone to the guard, who shook his head. A banknote went out through the bars. The guard nodded briefly. Pasqual took the short note from the Englishman and passed it to the guard. "Maybe it get there. Maybe not. *¿Quién sabe?*"

"Eight's my point," came Conomy's voice from a dimly lit corner. "Eighter from Decatur. Come on, dice!" A clicking sound, then: "Another buck, Jonesy. Pay me. Shoot five. Come on, babies. Papa's pets. Wish we could get that guard into the game. We'd have his uniform and side arms before taps sounded. Read 'em, Pig Iron."

"You damn' crook. Owe ya five."

And so they passed the evening, these men who stood in the shadow of the wall of death. Even Cartwright was shamed into some semblance of courage. Outside, the wondering guards listened to the laughter and jokes of the prisoners and shook their heads in puzzlement. "Loco *gringos*," they told one another.

The guard changed at daylight. Breakfast was brought in to the prisoners. Then Captain Ortega appeared with two squads of soldiers. The prisoners were filed out, manacled together. Out into a courtyard where several officers of evident high rank sat about a table.

A huge man in the center of the group read from a legal-looking paper, his guttural words falling on a heavy silence. He spoke in broken English.

No levity here. To a man, the prisoners felt the gravity of their position. Also, it was borne home to the Americans, that feeling of a helpless foreigner in a strange land. They were wholly at the mercy of these men who sat in judgment, guided in their judicial authority by half facts.

The huge man finished speaking. Then, upon the ominous silence, came the sharp challenge of a guard. The next moment a tall, gray-mustached man in immaculate flannels stepped into the enclosure and bowed formally. The Mexican officers rose and saluted with an air of deference. Then the man in flannels came forward, his unsmiling eyes fixed on the prisoners. His gaze finally fastened on the unshaven face of Tommy Atkins.

"God save us, Dick! Devil take me, old chap! You?"

"A bit the worse for wear, Randy, old lad." Atkins smiled. "But it is I, nevertheless. Beastly mess, what?"

"Rather. Rebel and all that, they tell me. I say, something's a bit twisted, eh?"

"Rather. I say, Randy, would you mind

extinguishing the cigar? As prisoners, we're not allowed the weed, and it's fairly overwhelming, if you follow me." Atkins smiled wanly, then adjusted the wounded arm in its crude sling. "Could you appeal in any way to these fellows? Tell 'em they're a bit hasty in their judgment, and all that? We weren't fighting their men or their country, Dick. Fact is, we succeeded in breaking up a revolution."

Beneath the light air of Atkins, MacLane caught an under drift of something else. Something that Atkins had buried and had but now unearthed. Something that was pinching the big Englishman's heart. The hurt of it was in his eyes.

"It's devilish cheeky of me to beg your aid, Randy," he went on. "But my friends stand in a grave position. Personally I'd have never appealed to you. You must understand that?"

"Quite, Dick. May I take this opportunity to say that you're no end of a damn' fool? Burying yourself while your friends hunted the earth and seven seas for you. I've mail for you . . . several letters. We were discussing you only last evening. By the way, is there some fellow named Conley or Conoley or some such name, with you?"

"Conomy?"

"Righto. Beastly memory for names. Know the chap?"

"Rather. Conomy, take your post."

Conomy saluted. "Now what have I done?" he asked a little belligerently.

The British consul smiled and drew a breath of relief. "Friend of yours has been making inquiries. Colonel Kirby. We dined together on his yacht last evening. He was coming over, but. . . ."

"Oh, damn your gun and your password," snapped a big voice from beyond the patio somewhere. There came sounds of a brief scuffle. Then a ruddy-faced giant came into the patio, carrying a bayonet in one hand and a rifle in the other. Behind him trotted a diminutive guard, sputtering broken English.

"Kirby!" gasped MacLane.

"Mac, or I'm drunk again. What the hell's all this? Conomy, you big bum, what's the rumpus?" He swung about on the guard. "Here's your toys, kid. Now trot along, and the next time you see an officer, be military."

Kirby threw a careless salute at the Mexican officers who squirmed a little uneasily. Then the big colonel spotted Cartwright.

"You, eh? Looks like a house fell on you, Cartwright. Quite a little family gathering.

I want you, Cartwright. Got papers to take you out, too. General Gonzales, this is the man I spoke of last evening at dinner. Whelp of the old he-wolf that we brought down in his trick battleship. Now what's the charges against these men here?"

"Inciting a revolution, Colonel."

"Somebody's all wet!" snapped Kirby. "Turn 'em loose. I'll vouch for 'em. You have under arrest here Colonel Atkinson of Great Britain, who is a British peer. Major Stuart MacLane . . . yeah, *major,* Mac, you idiot. Captain Jones of the former *Harriet Anne* and now under arrest on a U.S. federal charge that don't mean a damn' thing except extradition and a reprimand. Sergeant Conomy, of the U.S. Intelligence Department, and Pasqual Goldberg. Conomy, how does Goldberg stand?"

"Ace high, Colonel."

"Then he comes along." Kirby grinned. "Turn loose his soldiers."

"*¡Santa María!*" exploded Ortega. "But you cannot! They are rebels!"

"Rebels, hell! Get some spectacles, son. These boys don't want your country. I'll vouch for 'em all. General Gonzales, enlighten this gent before he throws a hydrophobia fit all over the place."

"This gentleman is of the International

Intelligence Department," explained the general to the fuming Ortega. "He is, to the American side, what your father is to Mexico. There has been some bad mistake somewhere."

"I say, Randolph," said Kirby, grinning, "looks like another little dinner party aboard the boat this evening. You've located your black sheep and I've found mine. Say, what the devil were you idiots doing, anyhow, when old Cartwright began his big push? You surely didn't think you could lick 'em and get all bitten up by the patriotic bug. Anyhow, not Pasqual Goldberg. Come clean, you renegades. What was it, gold?"

"You 'ave said it," admitted Pasqual with a shrug of his slim shoulders. "But son-of-a-gon, somebody 'ave get there first. Where I put that gol', she ees there no more. Ees gone."

"From the fort at Diablo Lake?" Kirby grinned.

"¡Sí, sí! You know about that gol'?"

"Sure. Caught 'em right at this port. One Mexican and ten of Cartwright's men. They were bringing it out with mules. The Mexican mentioned you as he was dying."

"Hees name?"

"José Lopez."

Pasqual nodded. "*Sí.* I knew he would sell hees map to Cartwright, also. A smart one, thees José Lopez."

"But not too smart," said Kirby. "My men nabbed 'em as they were taking the stuff out to one of Cartwright's boats. Who is the legal owner of that gold, anyhow?" He paused, then answered his own question. "The government of Mexico. But if you're hard up, I think we can arrange to get you gents a cut of it. You sure nipped a sweet revolution in the bud."

"How about gettin' off these bracelets, Colonel?" asked Conomy, shaking his heavy manacles.

Gonzales unlocked them himself. By some oversight the eagerly apologetic and wholly dazed General Gonzales also released Lee Cartwright.

Like a flash Cartwright whirled and bolted from the exit. Cartwright disappeared. Suddenly several shots rang out, outside along the street. Gonzales shrugged as the echo of the last shot died away.

"I am afraid, *Señor* Kirby," said the Mexican general, "that the *Señor* Cartwright has had the bad misfortune to be shot very dead."

"Just as well, for him," said MacLane, a little huskily. "He was due to be tried for the murder of Campbell."

"He'll be meeting his father," said Kirby in a quiet tone, "if there is a hereafter for such a man." Then, answering the question in MacLane's eyes, he finished quietly: "Old man Cartwright committed suicide sometime last night. Couldn't face the disgrace of discovery."

XII

That night, aboard the yacht that belonged to Colonel Kirby but in reality was used as a coast patrol boat to maintain international peace between two nations that were being preyed upon by such men as Cartwright, the party gathered for a banquet. Stuart MacLane read and re-read many times the thick letter that Kirby handed him after he had bathed.

"She's waiting, Kirby? For me?"

"Yes, you idiot. At San Francisco. That's only the sixth time I've told you. Want it in writing and witnessed before a notary? Where's Atkinson?"

"Gone ashore to cable London. Never saw a man so happy. Poor devil, he'd been eating his heart out over the fact that he loved another man's wife and she loved him. The husband, you see, was an officer of his battalion. A damn' rotter, so Randolph told me. But, you savvy, still her husband. Old families and so on. So Atkinson runs away before there's a scandal to blacken her name. Fortunately fate steps in and the woman's husband gets killed in an auto wreck."

"Another use for the automobile." Kirby nodded. His face softened a moment. He slapped MacLane's shoulder, turned abruptly toward the cabin door. "Seen Conomy? Listen and you'll hear him."

From above on the after deck came the big voice of Conomy. "Shoot a fin, General Gonzales. All of it? Atta boy. Come on, you freckled babies. Did 'er! Cleaned? Ten against that hat. Done. Come on, bones!"

"Conomy will win the whole Mexican army off Gonzales with those trick dice." Kirby grinned. "He's got everything the general's staff owned but their undershirts. Now about that girl in Frisco, Mac. Did I tell you she was . . . ?"

There was a little, husky catch in MacLane's laugh as he heaved a dusty boot up the companionway.

"Mess call, you lovelorn yokel!" called Kirby.

"Coming, Colonel." And he smiled happily at a little ivory miniature in a leather case on the dressing table. In a softer voice he added: "Coming, Betty Lou."

Wanted Men

I

"A Friend"

It was close to sundown when the posse pulled into the Figure 8 Ranch. They had been down in the badlands two weeks, rounding up the Long Jake bunch of rustlers. Now they were returning to Chinook, and stopped at the Figure 8 Ranch at the head of the cedar brakes. They pulled up at the corrals and swung stiffly from their saddles. The saddle horses and pack horses that carried their beds and camp outfit were gaunt and sweat-marked. The men were bearded, and their bloodshot eyes and grim mouths showed the strain of the past two weeks.

The boy, wide-eyed with excitement, watched them as they dismounted. He had just finished milking and was turning the milk cows out of the back corral. He saw that one man did not get off his horse. He sat in his saddle, a cold cigarette in one corner of his wide mouth, a half grin on his homely, red-whiskered face. The boy saw that his feet were tied under the belly of his horse, and that he wore handcuffs.

Now old man Haddock came hobbling from the bunkhouse, a squat, goat-whiskered, overalled old cowman with one game leg. The boy crouched behind the calf shed. No use letting old Haddock catch sight of him, or it might mean another quirting.

"Only ketch one?" called old Haddock in that voice of his that always seemed like a snarl. He pointed his heavy cane at the tall man with whiskers and hair the color of rusted steel. "Twenty men a-drawin' taxpayers' good money for two weeks, then a-showin' up with one uh the danged hoss thieves! *Pah!*"

The tall, gaunt-faced sheriff eyed the old cowman with undisguised displeasure. He jerked a gloved thumb toward two horses that bore burdens wrapped in bloodstained tarpaulins, lashed across the saddles.

"Long Jake an' Hogan," he said briefly, then turned his back on Haddock.

The grizzled old cowman jerked at his whiskers and bit off a piece of plug tobacco. "Who's this 'un on the hoss?" His heavy cane again pointed at the prisoner as he might have pointed a gun.

"Stranger." The sheriff jerked the saddle from his sweaty horse, and leaned his carbine against the corral. He gave a few brief orders to his men in a weary, drawling tone.

Now old Haddock hobbled over to where the tall prisoner sat his raw-boned roan horse. He peered up at the man from under his heavy iron-gray brows. "Who are ye, anyhow?" he roughly snarled.

The prisoner's wide mouth curved into a crooked line.

"I'm the king uh Siam in disguise. Put a pair uh horns on you, an' I'd swear you was an ol' goat we used tuh have down home. Yep, you're the spittin' image uh ol' Hardhead. He chawed tobacco, too."

With a quick snarl old Haddock swung his heavy stick, striking the defenseless man across the middle of the back. He would have struck again save for the fact that the lanky sheriff quickly jerked the cane from the gnarled old fist.

Old Haddock, for all his years, was a powerful man. The blow had been a vicious one. The man with the rust-colored hair and whiskers still grinned, but the gray eyes were hard and glittering.

"Leave my prisoner alone, Haddock,"

said the sheriff. "What kind of a man are you, anyhow, clubbin' a man that's tied up thataway?"

"He was insultin'!" Old Haddock's voice was thick with rage. "Called me a billy goat!"

"You've bin called a heap worse. Here's your cane. Git on to the house."

"This is my ranch. I go where I want. This ain't gonna help you none at the next election."

The sheriff turned his back on the snarling old cowman, and with his jack-knife he cut the rope that hobbled the prisoner's booted feet.

"Git down, red feller. I didn't know he was gonna hit you."

"I'd be proud to git just one long yank at them tobacco-streaked whiskers, Sheriff. Then I'd hang happy."

Old Haddock hobbled on back to the ranch house, muttering and cursing to himself.

The boy watched him go. He knew that, when he took the milk on to the kitchen, the old man would take out his snarling anger on him. Since he could remember, Haddock had beaten him, cursed him, starved him sometimes, and worked him twenty hours out of the twenty-four. With all his boy's heart he feared and hated that terrible old man with his club of a cane, and his heavy, shot-loaded rawhide quirt. The boy hated himself for not fighting back. He despised himself for not killing old Haddock. His thin, underfed body quivered now as he anticipated the whipping that old Haddock would give him when he took the milk over to the kitchen. He'd try not to yell when the quirt hissed and stung his back and legs that even now bore welts and unhealed scars from that ugly quirt.

"You'll hang, all right," the sheriff was telling the lanky prisoner, "but I never yet seen a man show any happiness at his own necktie party."

"I ain't hung yet, Sheriff. As the sayin' goes, there's sometimes a slip between the bottle and the lip. I never did have no love fer them rope neckties. When do we have grub pile, boss?"

"Directly the boys git the kitchen unloaded."

"We ain't havin' tuh swaller that ol' son-of-a-bitch's vittles, are we?"

"Not by a long shot, red feller. I'd rather go hungry."

"I'd plumb choke, honest, Sheriff." They laughed together.

The boy wondered how a man could laugh and joke when he was going to be hanged. His eyes shifted to the awkward, tarp-covered things that the men were taking from the two horses. Those blood-stained tarps hid the stiffened bodies of Long Jake and Hogan, the notorious rustlers. This joking, amiable-looking fellow with the rusty-colored hair and whiskers, and eyes that now were laughing, was an outlaw who had ridden with those dead rustlers. The boy had pictured outlaws as being surly, ugly-tongued men. But this fellow seemed good-natured.

Now old Haddock's harsh voice was bellowing:

"Hey, you Bart! Damn your triflin', no-account, lazy hide, git up here with that milk! Rattle your hocks, you consarned, time-wastin' young whelp!"

The boy grabbed up his milk pails. He had to pass the posse men and the two dead men and the grinning red-whiskered prisoner. The latter winked broadly at him as he passed.

"If he gits a-rarin', button, git a holt uh them ol' whiskers an' take your dallies. Drag the ol' cuss to death. Someday he'll git so mad he'll bite himself an' die uh hydrophoby."

The boy tried to grin back, but inside he was already cringing from the beating he expected.

But, save for an open-handed slap that made the boy's ear ring, he escaped punishment. Old Haddock limped back into his own private quarters to his eternal wicker-covered demijohn and his plug of tobacco. Later, perhaps, when the posse had gone, he would vent his spleen on the boy. But he was canny enough to know that beating the lad might stir up trouble. They might even take the boy away from him, and the authorities might get too nosey about how he happened to have this boy, and where the boy came from, and other questions that old Haddock did not wish to come up.

The cook, an undersize, meek-mannered, spindle-shanked little Chinaman, covertly slipped the boy a big piece of pie. He shared the boy's fear of old Haddock. Because Haddock knew that the Chinaman had been smuggled into the United States, he made the poor little cook believe that the punishment for illegal entry was long imprisonment.

The boy thanked him. "Much obliged, High Low." Then he slipped out of the kitchen and back to the corrals.

The posse cook was busy with his Dutch ovens. There were savory odors, the low-toned talk of the posse men. Now and then a laugh. The rattle of Dutch oven lids and the glow of the campfire in the dusk. Tarp-covered beds that smelled of horse sweat. The distant jingle of horse bells, where the cavvy grazed. Now the boy sighted the prisoner, his long, overalled legs stretched out on the ground, his raw-boned shoulders leaning against the corral. He was playing softly on a harmonica, and the metal handcuffs caught and reflected the firelight as his hands moved. His legs were bound at the ankles with stout rope. He had taken off his hat, and his thick, almost curly red hair was copper-colored in the firelight. Now and then his gray eyes let their glance stray toward the shadows beyond the firelight where lay the tarp-covered bodies of Long Jake and Hogan. He was playing "The Cowboy's Lament" — "For I'm a wild cowboy, and I know I done wrong."

To the boy it all seemed very tragic and sad. An aching lump came into his throat, and his eyes were stinging with unshed tears. Like when old Haddock had jerked his six-shooter and killed the boy's dog, and the boy had buried the dog after dark and hid the grave so that old Haddock couldn't find it.

The boy felt sorry for this rustler who sat there apart from the other men. When the firelight found the man's eyes, they looked soft and sad and sort of brave in spite of the sadness. The boy knew that the outlaw was playing his harmonica as a sort of farewell and funeral song to the two comrades who lay so still and stiff under the blood-stained tarps.

And now a queer sort of emotion gripped the boy. He felt that this man who was to hang was not bad. That between himself and the rusty-haired outlaw there was a strong bond of sympathy. Then came that impulse that was to change the whole life of the boy.

He backed away into the shadows, his bare feet making no sound. He made his way to the empty bunkhouse. It was roundup time, and the Figure 8 cowboys were away from the home ranch, branding the calves. The bunkhouse was in darkness, but the boy knew every foot, every inch of the place. He located a six-shooter where a cowboy had put it on a shelf. A box of .45 cartridges. Then he slipped out of the bunkhouse and down to the barn.

Old Haddock's two top horses were in

their stalls. The boy got two saddles and saddled the geldings that rubbed their velvety noses against his cheek. They knew and loved this boy even as they feared and disliked Haddock. They seemed to understand when he whispered to them to be awful quiet as he led them out the rear door of the long, log barn and down the creek to a clump of willows, where he left them.

He now made his way through the empty corrals. He could hear the clatter of tin cups and plates as the hungry men helped themselves at the Dutch ovens. Beyond the rim of firelight everything was pitch dark, for the moon would not be up for two or three hours. The boy crawled across the dark corral until he was directly behind the prisoner, who was eating, making an awkward job of it with his manacled wrists.

"Pssst." The boy's whisper was in the ear of the prisoner, who stiffened, then went on eating. "It's Haddock's kid. I'm shovin' my Barlow knife an' a gun alongside you. Got two horses hid down in the willer thicket below the barn. Take your time about leaving. Remember, I'll be a-waitin' there for you."

Then, as one of the posse men approached to get the prisoner's empty plate, the boy slid back into the black shadows.

II

"Freed"

The boy shivered, there in the darkness, as he crept away from the corral. He wondered what had made him do what he was now doing. Was he committing some terrible crime in helping that man to escape? The fellow was an outlaw, a horse thief, a cattle rustler. Still, he could not be much worse than old Haddock, whose reputation was tainted with unproven crimes. Haddock stole cattle from other outfits. He beat men in trades. He used all sorts of crooked ways to get land and water rights and grazing permits. Haddock was a slick old crook, no better than a man who stole openly.

And the tall, rusty-haired man didn't act like a thief. He laughed and joked and played music on his harmonica. His eyes were not shifty, like old Haddock's eyes.

The boy felt sorry about leaving High

149

Low. The Chinese cook had always been good to him. They were staunch friends. They both feared and hated old Haddock. Haddock's cowpunchers were a bad lot, too. They drank a lot of whiskey and gambled and quarreled. They kicked the boy around and laughed when Haddock put him doing chores that he hated. They, too, hated Haddock, but they drew good wages and had plenty of whiskey to drink. They stole for him, lied for him, fought for him. A scurvy lot of men, who could not hold jobs with respectable cow outfits. The Figure 8 had a tough name in Montana.

It was Haddock who had had the posse go after the Long Jake crowd. Some of Haddock's top horses had turned up missing, and he'd put up an awful holler.

The boy hoped there wouldn't be any more shooting. Killing men was bad business. He'd seen men killed right here at the Figure 8 Ranch. They bled a lot, and one of the men had suffered a long time before he died. Haddock had made the boy wait on the dying man. Haddock himself had done that killing. Over a poker game, although it was sworn to at court that it had been an accident.

Now the boy stiffened. He heard a man's voice. Brittle, hard, menacing. The red-haired feller's voice.

"Don't step out of the firelight, boys. I don't want to kill any of you, but I will if you crowd me. So long, Sheriff. Thanks fer your grub. Tell ol' goat whiskers I'll come back someday to pay him off fer what he gave me. OK, folks, *adiós!*"

The sound of a man running. Shots crashing everywhere. Now the tall outlaw was with the boy, flinging himself into the saddle, quick and easy in spite of the handcuffs. Then the boy and the red-haired outlaw were lying low along the necks of the two best horses in the Figure 8 remuda. Bullets snarled above them. The boy rode in the lead, the man following.

A mile. They slacked their headlong pace. The outlaw's voice came out of the velvet blackness of the night.

"By the time the night hawk gits the cavvy in, we'll be plumb into the badlands, button. Safe as if we were in jail. We'll eat breakfast on the south side uh the river. Boy, what made ya do what ya did?"

"I don't know. I . . . I didn't want to see you hung, for one thing. Then I wanted to run off from old Haddock anyhow."

"What's your name, son?"

"Bart."

"Bart what?"

"Just Bart, so far as I know." He added quickly: "I ain't no kin to ol' Haddock, I know that."

"*Hmm*. How old are you, boy?"

"Nineteen, I reckon. I'd be bigger an' stronger, only I don't eat much, an' I'm always lackin' fer sleep."

"*Hmm*. Well, Bart, we'll put some taller on your ribs, an', once we git where we're a-goin', we'll see that you ketch up on your shut-eye. You done Hank Plunkett a heap big favor this evenin', an' ol' Hank ain't the kind that fergits. Saved me from stretchin' rope, you did. Yep. They ketched me a-forkin' a Figger Eight hoss, an' that Haddock feller 'u'd uh spent the price uh a whole new remuda to hang me. I shore hate tuh see a boy like you a-travelin' with bad company like me, but you can't go back, and, if I don't take you along, them law fellers will pick ya up right now. That there sheriff is a wart hawg. Shore smoked Long Jake an' Hogan outta their holes. Well, let's put a few more acres uh Figger Eight range behind us, Bart. Know the trails?"

"I've rode 'em all a hundred times," said Bart eagerly, anxious to show his knowledge of the range.

"Then pick us the quickest 'un to the ol'

Missouri River, son. We're eatin' on yonder side at daybreak, heaven willin', and amen tuh that. Their horses is all played out. They ain't got a chance tuh ketch us. And if you like sourdough flap-jacks with chokeberry jelly and real steak, and mebbeso catfish and fried spuds and coffee that'll stand on its own laigs, then git your mouth all set and a-waterin', fer we're gonna tie into the best breakfast ya ever et. The duckin' we'll git a-crossin' the river will jest fix our appetites right. Lead the way, Bart. Now, let's git these bracelets knocked off me."

III

"Water Test"

It was before dawn when they rode down a bald adobe ridge and into the red willows and giant cottonwoods along the bottom land near the river. It was June, and the Missouri was running bank full. Dangerous even in broad daylight, and with a good water horse between a man's legs. To attempt the swim before daylight would be inviting a watery death. The outlaw and the runaway boy dismounted and loosened their saddle cinches. Hank made himself a cigarette, and the two sat there on the grassy bank above the river. There was, as the boy explained, a crossing down below, where, even at high water, there was only about fifty yards of real swimming.

"But we'll be carried downstream mighty near a mile, account of the current bein' swift. These is both good river horses."

The man nodded. The boy saw his wide mouth spread in a grim sort of smile.

"I crossed 'er last week, son. I come from yonder side."

"But I thought the Long Jake crowd all come from Milk River with them stolen horses," said the boy. "I heard the sheriff say so when they come past the ranch two weeks ago."

"So they did, I reckon, Bart. So they did. You're a smart 'un. And that's the way a boy had orter be. Eyes open and mouth shut. That's the ticket."

"I wasn't aimin' to be smart Alecky and nosey, mister," said the boy quickly.

"That's so, son," agreed the man. "You spoke without meanin' to ask what business I had crossin' the river from yonder side a week ago, when the rustlers come from up north way two weeks ago, and was pocketed by the sheriff's boys. Nope, ya never meant to be nosey, Bart. And I'd explain it to you how come I crossed the river, only we ain't outta this country as yet, and we might git ketched, you savvy? And if they ketched you, they might be askin' questions, you understand. In which case I'd hate to have you be a-lyin' fer Hank Plunkett. Lyin' is an almighty ornery habit to git into. Stick to the truth, son. Er

155

if you git in a tight, an' they question you, shut up like a barn door and say nothin'. Once in a purple moon there's an occasion where ya kin lie an' be plumb justified. Like if you lie to save the life of a friend er the good name of a woman. But mostly, Bart, stick like glue to the truth. Outside uh it bein' sinful an' plumb cowardly, lyin' gits a man into a heap uh trouble. One lie leads to fifty. Just like breedin' guinea pigs. Yep, I've knowed of a measly, puny, weak-kneed, sickly li'l' ol' two-for-a-penny lie tuh branch out till it growed into a plumb dangerous specimen. More laigs on it than a centipede er a devil fish. Lies is tricky thataway. They bites the hand as feed 'em, ya might say. So I don't want you to be havin' to lie fer Hank Plunkett." The rusty-haired, raw-boned, homely fellow took his large nose between thumb and forefinger and wiggled it back and forth. A habit of his that always amused and fascinated the boy.

They sat in silence there on the bank. Below them the muddy water lapped and gurgled and muttered under the high cutbank. Now and then there sounded the slap of a beaver's tail, the booming of a horned owl, the faraway yapping of coyotes. And just before dawn a wolf howled, long and mournfully. Bart wondered if the man were asleep, he sat so motionless, his back against a big cottonwood, his chin on his wide chest. But Hank Plunkett was not sleeping. His gray eyes were closed, to be sure, but his ears were strained to catch the faintest sound. The boy was too excited, too filled with the spirit of adventure, to close an eye. Hank broke a long silence. The sound of his voice made the boy jump a little. They both laughed at Bart's sudden start.

"I'm wonderin', son, if you ever run acrost a big Texas cowhand called Lee Waldron? Er mebbe he went under the name uh Lee Witten. Er he might be a-callin' himself Lee Watson? A big, good-lookin', black-haired cuss, with mean-lookin' black eyes like an Apache's."

"Not as I recollect, sir. But that ain't sayin' the man don't ride on this range. Haddock never let me off the ranch much. I never got to see any cowboys except the Figure Eight boys."

Dawn streaked the sky. Red smears across the gray. The birds were waking. Down below on the long sandbar they saw some blacktail deer coming down to water. There was the odor of wild roses and the muddy smell of the water below. A white-tail doe passed within fifty yards of where the man and boy sat. Then she caught their smell, and was gone like a flash.

"Another hour, son, and the crossin' will be good. Light's a little dim yet. The ol' river is plenty full uh snags that a man has to watch out fer. In about . . . shake a laig, boy, fer yonder comes hossbackers!"

A dozen riders were coming down the adobe ridge. Shadows moving against the drab clay of the long, bare ridge.

Cinches jerked tight, but not too tight. Hank looked with swift but expert eye at Bart's saddle cinch, shoving his hand between the cinch and the horse's ribs. For a horse tightly cinched can't do his best in bad water. Hank grunted his approval.

"You've swum 'er before, son?"

"Yes, sir."

They kept to the brush, bent low over their saddle horns. No use taking chances on being seen, although the men were still some distance away. Hank took his boots off and tied them to his saddle.

Bart led the way to the sandbar. Now they were in full view of the horsemen. A shout came up. Bart and Hank spurred into the muddy river. A moment, and the two horses were swimming for the south bank. Bullets sprayed around them, but the range was long, and the bullets were falling short. Both Bart and the man had now slipped out of the saddle and were swimming, hanging to the tails of their horses.

Bullets made little spurts on the muddy surface. But the shots were wild. In the half light the heads of two horses and two men were all but invisible against the background of the muddy water.

Bart's horse got hung up in a submerged snag that came down with the current. Probably a water-logged tree. The horse, terrified, kicked and struggled. Bart's face showed white against the swirling muddy water.

"Steady, son." Hank, behind the boy, had managed to swing his own horse a little downstream. "Let go now and swim fer me! That's it." His long arm shot out, grabbed Bart's forearm, and now the one horse towed its double burden shoreward. Bart was spitting and gasping for breath, dripping wet, his thin face almost blue, it was so bloodless. Hank's grip was like a steel band, as he held the half-drowned boy above water.

Hank's horse, a big sorrel with flax-colored mane and tail, was plowing through the water like a steamboat. Blowing through its nose with a rattling sound, swimming so high in the water that the lapping current barely wet the saddle skirts on the lower side.

Hank held tightly to the long tail with one hand, his other arm supporting the slim boy, who choked and sputtered and tried to grin.

Now the big horse found footing and lunged ashore. Twenty feet behind came Bart's big bay horse, snorting, swimming hard, its eyes wild with fear.

Ashore, Hank laid the half-drowned boy on the bank and caught the bay horse as the animal came ashore. Bart lay on his stomach, vomiting water. On the shore across from them the horsemen had pulled up. Now Hank knelt beside the boy, lifting him by his ribs, getting the water from his stomach and lungs.

"Ain't a one uh them jaspers got the sand to bust the ol' river, Bart. Nope, they ain't got the sand. They don't want us that bad, I reckon, boy. Feelin' better?"

Bart sat up dizzily. He nodded, forcing a grin. "I was scairt worse'n I was hurt. I ain't got nerve, that's all. If I ever did have any, ol' Haddock must 'a' whipped it outta me. I'm just a skinny, weak-backed coward."

The man chuckled, a queer look in his gray eyes. "How many times you ever tackled this river, son?" he asked.

"Twice. When the water was low."

"Kin you swim?"

"No, sir."

"*Hmm.* And so you figger ya ain't got sand, do you? See them gents on yonder bank? Well, I dunno as I'd call any of them fellers cowards. Like as not most of 'em kin swim, too. But they ain't hittin' this big ol' river this mornin'. I figgered, when we started acrost, that you could swim. Then, when you ketched in that snag, I saw you can't. No, boy, you ain't a coward."

"Kin you swim?" asked Bart suddenly.

"I kin dive like a feather an' swim like a rock. Nope, where I was brung up in Texas, in the windmill country, there wa'n't enough open water to float a cake uh soap. Me 'n' you 'u'd never make river hands."

He chuckled and poured the water from his boots. Then he took his harmonica from his pocket, and shook the water from it. From under his hat that had been crammed down to his ears he took the six-shooter Bart had given him.

"Everything all hunky dory, pardner. Now we'll play a tune tuh git ol' Annabelle dried out. Then we'll mosey along tuh them sourdough flapjacks an' steaks an' mebbeso catfish."

Whereupon this genial outlaw played a quick jig tune and cut a pigeon wing, to the amusement of the boy. Then they mounted, and this time Hank Plunkett took the lead.

Two hours later they rode along a dim trail into a box cañon. A cabin, a log corral, and stable. Some horses grazed in a little green pasture. Smoke came from the chimney. At Hank's shouted hail, the door of the cabin opened. A small, white-whiskered old man with long, white hair, came out, a long-barreled rifle in his hands.

"Hold your fire, Uncle Jim!" called Hank. "Swap that cannon fer a skillet an' commence to rattle 'er. We're both as ga'nt as bears in the spring."

IV

"A New Friend"

A queer little old fellow, Uncle Jim. With eyes as blue as a summer sky, and a smile that warmed the heart of the boy.

"So you're ol' Haddock's young 'un, are ye?" he drawled. His voice, like Hank's, was the soft speech of a Southerner. "I've heard tell about a boy he taken to raise some years ago, in the Colorado country. Did the old scalawag ever tell you about your own folks, sonny?"

"No, sir, he never told me nothing."

Uncle Jim snorted into his bushy white whiskers and began breakfast. The cabin was as neat as any woman's kitchen. His pots and pans and skillets were scoured until they shone. There was a red-and-white tablecloth on the pine table. The lamp chimney and lantern globe shone spotlessly. Snowy dish towels, curtains of blue denim. An old Navajo blanket on the

163

bunk. Plainly Uncle Jim was a neat man.

"Wipe your feet off, Hank Plunkett. Both of you peel off them wet duds and hang 'em ta dry. I'll rig ya out, even if I have ta wrop Hank up in that Injun blanket. Wet duds breeds colds and rheumatism. There's a nip uh good corn likker in the jug under my bunk, Hank. A leetle hot 'un will do the lad good, too. A toddy with nutmeg on the top. The lad looks peaked, Hank. Wet duds and an empty stomach. Looks like he'd never wropped hisse'f around a real meal uh vittles in his life. Leave him with me an' I'll git the wrinkles outta his stomach in jig time."

"I aim tuh let him stay here a spell, Uncle Jim. I didn't git all my business tended to on yonder side uh the river. Run into a snag." Hank, now stripped to the hide, as was Bart, and each with a blanket around him, they sat on homemade chairs, near the stove, for the day was cloudy and their swim had left them chilled in damp clothes.

Hank slapped his leg and chuckled, saying: "I shore knocked me over a real hornet's nest, Uncle Jim. I did, and no mistake, and only fer the button here, I'd uh stretched rope."

"How's that again?" The blue eyes under

the heavy white brows lost their laughter. The change startled the boy.

"I got picked up by the sheriff's posse. Long Jake and Mike Hogan was killed. The others made a getaway. I was doin' good till my horse hit a soap hole and somersaulted. Hit my skull on a rock, and I woke up with a headache and hand-cuffs on. We stopped at Haddock's tuh spend the night, and Bart here cuts me free and stakes me to a gun and a horse. I'm plumb in debt tuh the boy, Uncle Jim."

"I'd so reckon." Uncle Jim laid a strong, kindly hand on the boy's shoulder. "He's got a good eye in his head, Hank. And an upstandin' and honest manner. Good stock in him. Straight nose, good chin, a straight mouth, and wide-set eyes. Good blood there, er Uncle Jim Taylor is no judge uh humans. Now sip this toddy, sonny. It'll warm your innards so's this grub will taste like it orter. And when breakfast is done, into my bunk you go. And there you stay, lad, till there ain't no more sleep left in your system. He needs feedin', Hank, and rest. You won't know the boy in a month."

Bart felt a lump in his throat. This sort of kindness was a new experience. He felt his eyes sting, but fought back a desire to cry. Hank looked at the boy covertly, winked at Uncle Jim, and tapped his harmonica against the palm of his hand. Then he played some lively tunes, and did an Indian dance that had both the boy and Uncle Jim laughing. His red hair and whiskers, his large, misshapen nose, the gaudy blanket, made an amazing picture. Then he grabbed the butcher knife and went through the motions of scalping their host.

"A born idiot, son," said the chuckling old man. "He'll never git his full senses if he lives ta be a hundred."

Hank wagged his nose and took another drink from the jug. The toddy made Bart feel warm and light-headed. Then came the breakfast. Steak as tender as chicken, broiled catfish, sourdough flapjacks, and thick chokeberry syrup. Coffee that was strong and black. Filled up, Bart dozed in his chair. But he tried to persuade Uncle Jim to let him wash the dishes. Hank picked the boy up and put him to bed. It seemed to Bart that sleep came instantly.

When the boy was asleep, Uncle Jim and Hank, the latter now wearing some misfit clothes, did the dishes. Then they went outside.

"Ye didn't hear no word uh Waldron? Never crossed his sign, Hank?"

"No. But he's over there somewheres. If that fool posse hadn't mixed me up with the Long Jake bunch, I might 'a' picked up Waldron's trail. But I run slap-dab into the mess. And I was in a bad fix when this boy helped me out."

"Now they think you're one uh Jake's crowd?"

"Shore certain. Ain't that the dog-gonedest luck? When things get quiet on yonder side, I'll tackle it once more. You'll kinda ride herd on the boy till I kin git him located somewhere safe from Haddock? Only for him, I'd like as not bin into a bad mess. The boy is shore in need of friends."

"He's found 'em, Hank. You know plumb well he's welcome here. And ol' Haddock won't be comin' here a-huntin' him, nei-ther. I done sent the ol' rascal word that, whenever he set foot on my land, he'd git a hide full uh lead. He knows better'n ta chance it. What's the boy's whole handle?"

"He don't know. Says all the name he knows is just Bart. Why?"

"Nothin', I don't reckon, Hank. Only why does a mean-hearted, close-fisted, ornery ol' rascal like Haddock take a four, five-year-old boy ta raise? Why does he keep him there, never lettin' the boy outta sight, ya might say, never lettin' the boy go ta town or talk ta outside folks? He's starved the boy, beat him, by the looks uh them welts on his pore skinny frame. He's kep' the boy like a dad-burned slave, Hank. Why? The boy ain't strong enough ta do a man's work. You might say he ain't bin worth his keep. There's somethin' behind it, I tell you. The lad reminds me uh somebody I've knowed, too. The way he holds his head. Kinda like a Thoroughbred colt that ain't begun ta develop yet. And them eyes that's neither gray nor brown, but a mixture. Hazel-colored eyes, wide-set. That black hair, and straight, thick black brows. Them sensitive lines around his nose and mouth. I've seen all them things on another man's face, somewheres. I'll recollect someday."

Hank nodded and grinned. Uncle Jim was great for mysteries. He was always figuring out some puzzle or another. Hank's tolerant grin brought a disgusted snort from the other man.

"Ya big, red-headed monkey."

Hank lowered the pair of field glasses through which he had been watching as the two sat on a rocky ledge that made a fine look-out point.

"Expectin' company today, Uncle Jim?"

"Not as I knows about. Somebody a-comin'?"

"Three men. I'll cache them two Figger Eight horses, then hide out. Holler if you need me."

V

"Followed"

The sound of voices woke the sleeping boy. Years with old Haddock had made a light sleeper out of Bart.

Bart, through the window, saw three men on horseback, talking to Uncle Jim, who stood there, a six-shooter in his hand, overalled legs braced wide apart. The three men were Figure 8 cowpunchers. An ugly-looking trio, all armed.

"We follered the horse tracks here, old man," said one of the three. "Two shod horses. Word come across the river that two Figger Eight horses crossed this mornin' early. The horses was stolen. We got orders to git them horses and a red-headed feller and ol' Haddock's kid. We mean business, you white-muzzled ol' rascal."

Bart picked up a shotgun that stood against the wall. The sight of that old man facing the three rough customers from the

Figure 8 outfit stirred something wild in the boy. He broke the gun to make sure it was loaded. Then he pulled open the door and stood beside the old man.

"You tell Haddock that when we git done with them horses, we might return 'em. You ain't takin' me back alive."

"Listen to the young rooster crow!" leered one of the three.

"His wings shore sprouted sudden. Listen, you young fool, the ol' man will whip you raw fer this. Git your clothes and come along."

"You heard the lad," said Uncle Jim slowly. "He ain't a-goin' back. But if you three specimens ain't movin' away from this place right sudden, you're goin' ta have bad luck. Git!"

"When I give the word," said the leader of the three, "we'll rush the ol' gray back an' the kid. We ain't goin' ta go back an' say an ol' coot an' Haddock's kid bluffed us."

Now a tall, raw-boned, rusty-haired man stepped from the brush. He wore a gun shoved into the waistband of his overalls, but his big, heavy hands hung free. There was a grin on his wide mouth, but his eyes were unsmiling and hard.

"Here's your horse thief," he drawled.

"Who feels lucky enough tuh try an' take me?" He kept walking toward the three mounted men, until he was at the stirrup of the glowering man who seemed to be the boss. Without turning his head, Hank called to Uncle Jim.

"Kill the first 'un that makes a bad move. I'm learnin' this long-coupled feller a music lesson."

With a cat-like leap he had vaulted up behind the saddle. His long, strong arms wrapped themselves about the man as the startled horse jumped, then whirled, pitching. The next moment Hank and the man in his embrace were thrown. Hank twisted in midair, like a trained acrobat, so that, when the two hit the ground, Hank's fall was broken by the big frame of the other man. The man's eyes rolled. He gasped for breath. Hank slapped him playfully as he sat astride the fellow.

Now Hank unbuckled the cowpuncher's belt and gun, and tossed it to Bart. Then he lifted the man to his feet, kicked him once or twice, and slapped his face with his hat.

"Fork that geldin' an' hit the grit, feller. Or I'll start drillin' air holes in your clothes. Your two *compadres* will be ketchin' up tuh ya soon. Drag it, bad feller!" Another kick, and the cowpuncher feebly climbed into his saddle.

"And now you two wicked varmints will either use them guns you're a-packin' or else throw 'em away here an' now. Bart, you ain't never killed a man, have you?"

"No, sir."

"You know these two jaspers. Did they ever rawhide you much?"

"Some."

"So I surmised, as the feller says. Well, button, that scatter-gun you're holdin' is loaded with buckshot. She's got two triggers an' two barrels. There's two uh these polecats here. While I'm admittin' they don't grade up so smart as targets, still an' all a man can't be so choosy at his fust killin'. Me 'n' Uncle Jim will swear it was self-defense. Billy the Kid was twelve years old when he killed his fust 'un. You're makin' sign now, Bart, along the outlaw trail. Kill 'em like ya'd blow the head off a black-diamond rattler. Shoot high, so's not tuh hurt their horses."

The boy's thumb passed across the twin hammers of the shotgun. His eyes questioned the genial red-haired outlaw. He wondered if Hank really meant what he was saying. Hank's face was hard to read. A red-whiskered, grinning face, but the eyes were cold. Now like a wet sponge across a slate, Hank's expression changed.

"Kill 'em, button."

Bart's eyes met Hank's cold, commanding stare. The two Figure 8 men had lifted their hands now, and their faces became tight-looking and bloodless. Bart questioned the rusty-haired outlaw with his eyes. Hank nodded grimly.

Bart put the double-barreled shotgun on the ground. He faced Hank Plunkett, his face white as chalk.

"I ain't a murderer," he said, his voice dry and toneless. "I can't cut 'er, sir, I reckon . . . I reckon I'm kinda white-livered."

The boy stood there, hands empty, straight-backed, ragged, his feet bare. There was an odd light in his hazel eyes as he faced the red-haired outlaw. Inside, he felt sick and trembling.

Hank took his large nose between thumb and forefinger, and wagged it thoughtfully. Then he looked at the two cowpunchers.

"Shed your guns, polecats, then drift. Make 'er fast. And thank this boy for your mangy lives."

When the two men had ridden away, leaving their guns there on the ground, Hank Plunkett came over to Bart and put a long arm across the boy's slim shoulders. Bart shrank a little from the man's touch.

"That wa'n't hardly fair tuh you, son. But I had tuh know just how far you'd go."

"Just a big, red-muzzled clown," growled Uncle Jim. "Uh course it wan't fair ta the boy, Hank. But he taken it like a Thoroughbred. Ye savvy what I mean by Thoroughbred, ya loose-jointed, grinnin' ape?"

"You called the card right, Uncle Jim. Bart, son, you've fell amongst evil men, but we'll do what we kin tuh shape your destiny, as the sayin' goes. I'll be leavin' you in the good care uh Uncle Jim, son. I got business on yonder side uh the river. Mebbeso, now and then, betwixt and between, we'll meet, occasional. Uncle Jim is here an' forever henceforth your guardian. I never meant for you tuh kill no man, Bart. Killin' is what the feller says . . . a bad habit, an' downright sinful. Dally your rope onto what wisdom Uncle Jim spouts forth of an evenin'. Don't miss 'er, nary a word, fer he's got more hoss sense and book learnin' under that white hair than twenty preachers an' professors. I'll be a-sayin' so long tuh you now, Bart. The good Lord a-willin', we'll meet up soon. Would you care about shakin' hands, Bart?"

The grin had left his homely face. The gray eyes were soft, pleading.

Gravely they shook hands. Uncle Jim had gone back into the cabin.

So it was that the boy Bart stood there alone, watching the red-haired outlaw ride away alone. Bart saw him ride out of sight, then he went back to the cabin. He found the old man packing his few belongings.

"Run the hosses into the corral, Bart. Looks like we have ta be movin' on."

"But this is your home, Uncle Jim. And it's my fault you're movin'."

"It ain't no more my home than it is yourn, son. Jest a stoppin' place. An' it ain't your fault we're a-pullin' stakes. I'll be showin' you a green spot in Wyomin' that cheats this ta death. We'll drift on into Colorado, Utah, New Mexico. We'll be seein' country, Bart."

Uncle Jim was like a schoolboy beginning vacation. He hummed and whistled through his teeth as he and Bart packed up.

"Will we be seein' Hank Plunkett?" asked the boy.

"Hank? Shore, if they don't hang 'im. Throw your hull on that dun-colored hoss, Bart. He'll pitch a few, but he don't mean a thing. Jest high-speerited. He'll carry you

176

from Alberta ta Chihuahua without turnin' a hair. Made ta order fer a light load like you be. The bed goes on that G Dot paint pony. The grub goes on that wide-backed sorrel that is tryin' ta hunt pancakes in the kyack box. Kittles, skillets, an' such we tie on that grulla mule. Watch his hind laigs, Bart, fer he's as wicked as sin. Hosshoes and muleshoes an' the odds an' ends we puts on that one-eyed blue roan. Look at 'em waitin'. They knows it's time we was hittin' the trail. Every last one of 'em knows more'n me an' you put together. Bart, them fool hosses makes life a shore-enough burden. They bully a feller till he kain't see straight. Wiser'n owls, foxy as coyotes, them rascals. Any one of 'em kin pack a man ten miles ahead uh the fastest sheriff. I don't own a pair uh hobbles ner a picket rope. That dun pony an' this big brown I ride kin move along any man's trail on the blackest night, an' never make a stumble. All hackamore hosses. Never had a bit in their mouth. Now he'p me throw this diamond hitch. Bart, we're a-movin' yonderly."

Pack animals all loaded. Saddles cinched. Bart's buckskin pony bucked a few jumps, then came back to camp on a trot, the boy grinning happily. Already he

177

had become friendly with Uncle Jim's horses and the mule. The old fellow was as happy as a king. He took a nip at the jug, then lashed it on top of the bed. Together, the pack animals stringing out ahead, the mule in the lead, they quit the box cañon.

Bart asked no questions. The old cowpuncher volunteered no information. So they climbed out of the cañon and followed a dim trail westward toward the Wyoming country.

Bart kept thinking of Hank Plunkett, riding alone.

VI

"Alone"

Days and nights followed, when Uncle Jim and Bart rode their twisted trail into the Wyoming country. A broken, often trackless trail that no pilgrim could have found. Mostly they traveled mornings and late evenings, and sometimes after dark. Once, when Uncle Jim saw something or someone through his field glasses, a sign that spelled danger no doubt, they traveled all night, and made no fire the next day, although it was drizzling rain and cold, and they were soaked to the bone. For they were in a mountain country, and the altitude chilled the rain that swept down out of a gray sky.

But mostly the weather was fair. There was an abundance of water, and the feed was good. Cattle grazed on the hills. They killed a sucking yearling and gave most of the meat to some Indians they met. Uncle Jim talked the sign language and knew the

179

ways of Indians. He bought moccasins and a buckskin shirt for Bart, who was barefooted and all but shirtless. In his fringed buckskin, the boy looked almost like an Indian, with his straight black hair, his heavy black brows, except for the hazel eyes set in a tanned face that was beginning to lose its pinched look. Uncle Jim eyed the boy with sidelong glances as they rode along, studying Bart's profile and the manner in which he held his head.

On several occasions they camped with other men. Silent-lipped, hard-eyed, heavily armed men who called Uncle Jim by name. Bart asked no questions, spoke when he was spoken to, and made himself useful around camp. He knew these men they met were outlaws. Yet they seemed no different from other men. A trifle more spare of tongue, perhaps, and they looked at a person with suspicious eyes, but they were not bullies or foul-mouthed, like old Haddock and the Figure 8 crew of rowdies.

When the old man and boy camped alone, Uncle Jim talked a good deal. He told Bart many things about camping, about following a trail, about hiding your sign from men who were following you. He entertained the boy with stories of the old cattle trails. Stories of Texas and the

Rangers, of Tombstone and old Santa Fé, of Dodge City, and other wild towns along the old cattle trail. Colorful yarns about the buffalo hunters and Indians and government scouts. Of cowmen, sheriffs, rustlers, killers. And through his rambling tales was woven a golden thread of philosophy that Uncle Jim had worked out. He revealed an astounding knowledge of the Scriptures.

"String your bets with the Almighty, son. When a man splits the blankets with his God, he's a-headin' on a bad trail."

He carried a small, leather-bound Bible, which he kept carefully wrapped in a canvas jacket, and, when the light was good, he often read passages from the Book. It pleased him when Bart asked questions. His answers were homely and roughly hewn, but nearly always held the meat of truth.

Now and then Bart asked about Hank Plunkett. Did Uncle Jim reckon anything had happened to Hank?

"Hard ta say, son. I reckon not. Hank's a good hand at lookin' after his scalp." But if anything had happened, they'd be getting word. The outlaw trail had its ways of passing along news.

For two weeks — going on three weeks

— they were camped on Powder River. Uncle Jim left Bart in camp, and went to town for some grub.

"If I ain't back by tomorrow night, pack up and head south, lad," he instructed the boy in his kindly manner.

He rode away on the big brown horse, leading the fat sorrel, with empty kyack boxes tied to the pack saddle.

Bart, alone in camp, felt strange and uncomfortable. He knew that, for the past three days or so, Uncle Jim Taylor had been worrying about something. He had kept a sharp look-out for strangers, and had avoided meeting any riders.

Bart cleaned his carbine and six-shooter. He had little appetite for the food he cooked, although the prairie chicken was fried to a king's taste, and the Dutch oven biscuits were light and palatable.

That night he spread his bed in a brush thicket that was well hidden. But he could not sleep. He lay on his back, watching the stars. His guns were alongside his head. He thought of old Haddock and Hank Plunkett and that tall, quiet-tongued sheriff from Chinook.

Uncle Jim had inferred that, if all went well, he would be back at camp sometime during the night. If he did not show up by noon, Bart was to get things in shape to break camp. If he were not back at dark the following night, Bart was to hit the trail, avoid meeting anyone, and keep moving along the route Uncle Jim had so often described, crossing the North Platte and following the Continental Divide. In the boy's mind were the descriptions of places to stop, the names of men he might meet and be free to talk to, towns to avoid.

Bart could not help but wonder just what sort of a desperate game Uncle Jim Taylor and Hank Plunkett were playing. They acted like outlaws; they knew the outlaws who rode this forbidden trail from Montana to Mexico. Yet it was hard to associate a carefully read Bible and the bark of a rifle. Uncle Jim did not have the earmarks of a badman. He drank sparingly, swore seldom, and spoke of womanhood in a tone of profound respect, almost reverence. He held honesty and truthfulness as sterling virtues. He told Bart time and again that a man whose spoken word was not as good as a bond was no real man. Those things, so Uncle Jim told the boy, were part of a real man's code of honor. And a man without a code of honor is worse than dead. He inferred that Hank Plunkett was a man of honor. Yet Bart had heard him condemned as a horse thief.

Bart's boy's mind was crammed with bewildering thoughts and conjectures. He could not think evil of Uncle Jim and Hank Plunkett. Uncle Jim, with his worn Bible and his homely philosophy. Hank Plunkett, with his grin and his love of a joke and his harmonica.

It was sometime in the middle of the night when the boy's ears caught the sound of shod hoofs. He woke from his dozing, his hand covering the butt of his big six-shooter, his heart pounding fast against his ribs. There was no moon. The stars hung low in the black sky. Now his throat seemed to throb with every pulse beat. Two men sat their horses there in the little clearing alongside the riverbank. Shadowy shapes in the black night. One of them stepped down off his horse. He kicked Uncle Jim's rolled bed there by the kyack boxes.

"His bed's rolled up. Looks like he's gone to town."

"Reckon the kid's with him?"

"That'd be my guess. Might look aroun' to make certain. But I'd make the guess that he ain't lettin' the button outta his sight. He's as foxy as a wolf, is Jim Taylor."

"What's to keep him from hidin' in the

brush, watchin' us right now. A rolled-up bed don't exactly mean the ol' son-of-a-bitch has quit camp."

"Scared, are you?"

"Not exactly. Cautious, that's all. Jim Taylor is bad medicine with a gun, that's all."

"Kick around them bushes. I'll poke around on the other side uh his camp. Kill whatever moves. But it's my bet the ol' son-of-a-bitch is in town an' taken the kid with him. That kid's worth money, or Haddock wouldn't be postin' no such reward. Jim Taylor ain't the man to let that much money stay in camp when he goes to town. If the button is worth one thousand to Haddock, he's worth that much to Jim Taylor, savvy?"

Bart slipped into the blackest shadows. His moccasined feet made no noise. His slim frame burrowed into the underbrush. From his hiding place he listened to the two men as they prowled about. The voices of the men were familiar. One he knew to be the big Texan called Pecos, who ran the Figure 8 roundup. The other was an ugly-tempered man they called Missouri.

Shivering a little, his jaws clamped until his ears ached, Bart lay there in the dense underbrush, his gun in his hand. More than a few times Pecos had slapped and cuffed the boy. Missouri was a tobacco-chewing, ungainly bully, ugly when he was drunk, which was most of the time. A bad pair. Bart heard them beating the brush, heard them talking. Pecos was smashing his way through the brush. He stood almost within arm's reach of the hidden Bart. He was breathing heavily and cursing in a muttered undertone. He stood there now, motionless, in the darkness. Bart's heart pounded until he was afraid the big Texan would hear the thumping of it against his ribs. Why was the man standing there? Did he know where Bart was hidden? Had he found the two blankets rolled up and hidden in the heavy underbrush? Bart gripped his heavy six-shooter. Horribly afraid, yet determined to fight it out with these two big renegades, he waited.

He heard the sound of a cork pulled from the neck of a bottle. A gurgling sound. Pecos coughed a little as the strong whiskey bit his throat. Then he moved on.

"Might as well head fer town, Missouri."

"We're wastin' time here, Pecos."

The jingle of their spurs. The swish of their chaps. Now they rode away into the night. Bart was alone once more.

Indecision pulled the boy's mind in different directions. Should he saddle up and beat these two men to town? Or should he obey Uncle Jim's emphatic orders and stay at camp? Should he pack up and hit the trail tonight? Or should he do as Uncle Jim had told him to do, stay here until tomorrow night? Uncle Jim's orders had been plain. He had told Bart to stay clear of town. Plain as two and two. Haddock had posted a reward for Bart. The boy reckoned that Uncle Jim knew all about that reward.

Impulse, loyalty to the old man, urged Bart to saddle up his line-backed dun horse and beat those men to town. Obedience to Uncle Jim's orders commanded him to stay here. Better follow those orders.

Bart crouched there in the darkness, alone, miserable because he did not know what was the right move to make, fearing for the safety of Uncle Jim Taylor, yet obedient to the old cowpuncher's orders. Bart sat there, a little chilly from the night air, his carbine across his lap, his six-shooter in its holster. Hour after hour, until dawn broke across the sky. His stomach felt like an empty, aching thing that could never again hold food. His eyes burned from those hours of staring into the black night. He was shivering with cold and dread of what he feared might have happened in town. He hated himself for being unable to make a man's decision. He called himself a coward, a weakling. Why hadn't he called those two big toughs, shot it out with them, then and there? Why hadn't he beaten them to town and warned Uncle Jim?

I'm just a weak fool, Bart told himself, *a thick-skulled, sandless kid.*

He made a fire and cooked breakfast, but ate without tasting the food. Morning dragged away, and, when the sun showed noon, Bart began packing up. His heart was like a lump of lead. He felt that Uncle Jim would not return today or tomorrow. Perhaps never. And Bart held himself to blame. He had let an old man carry the burden that should have been borne by younger shoulders. He had quit Uncle Jim in a tight place. With heavy heart Bart carefully packed the kyack boxes and fixed Uncle Jim's bed for packing. In the old fellow's war sack was the Bible in its handmade canvas jacket. Bart felt that he was packing the belongings of a man dead.

At sundown, Bart loaded the pack animals. He saddled his horse and fought back the tears that stung his eyes, swallowed again and again the aching lump that choked his throat.

And as darkness fell, the boy rode away from the camp on Powder River. Alone. The pack animals stringing out ahead. All alone. Because Uncle Jim had told him to pull out at that hour. To head southward and keep moving.

"Head yonderly, lad. Foller where that grulla mule leads ya. He knows the trail better'n most men. Camp where he stops, Bart. Keep a-goin' till ya hit New Mexico. Ta that ranch on the upper Animas. When the right men ask questions, give 'em true answers. When the other kind git curious, know nothin'. I'll be a-ketchin' up with ya somewhere if I'm alive. You're young an' the whole world's spread out fer ya like turkey an' cranberry sauce. Me, I'm old and bin a-cheatin' the graveyard many a year as it is. Keep a-driftin', Bart, till ya hit that ranch at the upper end uh the Animas. Tell 'em my name. Now I'll be a-leavin' ya, Bart. So long."

So Bart left Powder River. Alone. With a leaden lump in his boy's heart, he headed yonderly into a strange country, following the grulla mule toward New Mexico.

He watched a star fall, and wondered if there could be any truth to that old saying that, when a star falls, it is a sign that a friend has just died.

VII

"Flying Fists"

Brown's Park, in the Colorado country, was a spot where hunted men stopped. Bart had been alone now for a week. His grub supply had run low, and he had been living for five days on straight meat and Dutch oven bread. His hair had grown long, and a boyish-looking growth of black beard gave him the appearance of being older. His frame was filling out, and his muscles were long and hard and sinewy. Tanned a deep bronze, he looked more than ever like an Indian, with his black hair and his buckskin clothes. Following the grulla mule that had picked the trail without faltering, from Powder River into Brown's Park country, Bart came alone.

It seemed to the boy that he had aged ten years in the past week. The days were empty for him, although he used every hour in watching the ever-changing country, noting landmarks, using every trick and every bit of trail craft taught him by Uncle Jim. And he had learned much from the grulla mule and the G Dot paint pony and his line-backed buckskin gelding. Because Uncle Jim had told him how a man could learn a heap from a horse, and that the grulla mule had the wisdom of ten horses. By watching the long, fuzzy ears of that mouse-colored little mule, Bart could tell when they were near any men or horses. Nor did he need to haze the mule off the trail and into a hiding place. That mule would voluntarily quit the trail and bush up, standing, motionless, for as long as half an hour sometimes.

Bart was learning things. Thrown on his own, he did the best he could to follow Uncle Jim's teaching.

Several times he had sat on a high butte, and with his field glasses had watched the lights of a nearby cow town. Bart had never been in a big town. The twinkling lights had beckoned. His blood pounded swiftly at the thought of riding into a real town. In his pocket was money Uncle Jim had given him. A roll of greenbacks that tallied up to almost $1,000. Bart dreamed of buying some clothes. Boots and a hat and a flannel shirt and new overalls. A

paper sack full of stick candy and pepper-
mint and wintergreen candy. A silk neck
scarf to tie around his neck. A cigar with a
gold band. Bart had never smoked a cigar.
He pictured himself walking up the street
with a cigar in his hand, spurs jingling on
his new boots, hat slanted across one eye.

But Uncle Jim had told him to steer shy
of towns. Bart would go to his blankets in
the brush, fighting off the fear that tried to
grip his heart. He thought of Uncle Jim as
a friend who has died. Hank Plunkett and
his harmonica seemed like a dream. The
boy would kneel at night and pray to God
in homely, boyish words, for Hank and
Uncle Jim. Then he would ask God to help
him be a man.

Bart was glad when he pulled in at
Brown's Park. A dozen men were camped
there. The boy asked for baking powder.
The men who were gathered around him
exchanged looks. To ask for baking powder
was giving the password that he was one of
them. They eyed him cautiously.

"Who told you to come here, button?"

"Uncle Jim Taylor. I'm headin' for New
Mexico."

"Which bein' the case," said a man with
the blackest eyes the boy had ever seen,
"you might as well keep a-movin'. Us boys

is busy, and the only nurse near here that could tend to you is some miles distant. Roll along, button."

"Uncle Jim Taylor told me to stop here."

"Well, ain't that just nice? Told you to stop here, did he? Well, I'm tellin' you different, young feller. You're rollin' along."

"That's Jim Taylor's mule," said one of the men. "Them's his hosses."

The man with the black eyes whirled like a panther. His white teeth showed as his thin lips curled in a snarl.

"I didn't ask your opinion. This kid drifts on. I'm boss here. Drag it, button, while you're able to move."

"I wouldn't stay now," said Bart, "if you paid me a million. I don't stop where I ain't wanted. I don't need to be told so, either. I'm just a kid, shore, but kids grow up, and, when I git growed, I hope to meet up with you, mister. Because I wouldn't treat a mangy dawg as you're treatin' me."

Bart was astounded at his own words. Something inside him was burning like fire. His hand was on his gun, his narrowed eyes were staring hard into the black eyes of the man who stood there, thumbing the hammer of a .45. Bart felt the deadliness of the man. But he did not flinch under the black stare.

"Go get your growth, button, then make that fight talk."

"Yes, sir. That's my intentions."

Bart quit Brown's Park, his nerves on edge. He made his camp that night in a hidden spot. Supper over, he cleaned his skillet and dishes, then saddled the dun-colored horse and headed for town. But before he left, he practiced drawing his gun. The gun had been emptied of cartridges. For an hour Bart practiced drawing and snapping the long-barreled six-shooter. Then he loaded the gun and saddled up.

Following the teachings of Uncle Jim, Bart's first move in town was to care for his horse. The night was half gone, the hour being two or more hours past midnight. Yellow lights illuminated the street, making spots in the darkness. Bart had given the man at the barn $5 to grain his horse and fill the manger with good hay. He had hidden his carbine in a manger, and covered it with hay. For Uncle Jim had told him that a man on dangerous business in a strange town does certain things, like hiding his Winchester and caring for the horse that might have to pack him quickly out of trouble.

"Feed your hoss keerful. Grain. Some

hay. A leetle water. Enough ta satisfy a hoss' thirst, but not enough ta make him loggy. Put your saddle gun where no man knows where ya put 'er. Keep your saddle on your hoss. Loosen the cinch, so's he gets his wind an' his grain all proper. Always hide your saddle gun in the hay. Know that barn so's you kin git your hoss in the dark. Lightin' matches in the dark thataway is a mighty onhealthy habit."

Now Bart walked up the street. A strange figure in his moccasins and buckskin shirt, and his straight black hair that hung almost to his shoulders. He wore his six-shooter low on his right flank, the holster tied by a thong around his leg. Even old Haddock would have had to look a second time to recognize this bronzed, lean figure as the skinny, pinched-faced boy who had run off about a month ago.

His appearance excited no curiosity. There were men of all types here in this booming cow town and mining camp. Cowboys, miners, a sprinkling of trappers and freighters, gamblers, drifters of all kinds.

Gambling was wide open. Barrooms crowded. Stores and restaurants filled with customers. Plenty of gold money in circulation. Whiskey fifty cents a drink. Flour

$10 a sack. Haircut a dollar. A rough, free-handed crowd. Fiddles squeaked, accordions wheezed. A pasty-faced man played a tin-pan piano, his eyes almost closed, a cigarette hanging limply from his mouth as he sang songs of lost sweethearts and white-haired mothers. "The Baggage Car Ahead" and "You Made Me What I Am Today". Women with hard eyes and red slippers. Dancing with flannel-shirted miners and booted cowboys.

Bart had never seen a real town. His eyes missed the tawdry side, the tarnished gilt of it. To him the lights, the music, the crowds spelled life. He gaped at the store windows. He wanted to go in and buy a pair of boots and a red flannel shirt and a bright neck scarf. He wanted some candy. A haircut with grand-smelling tonic. A shave, even. Bart's hair had never been cut by a barber. He had never had a real shave. He wanted all those things, but a strange, overwhelming timidity held him back. He felt that everyone was staring at him. His face felt hot and sweaty. His hands seemed too big, and he did not know what to do with them. If only Uncle Jim or Hank Plunkett were with him. But he was alone, a plumb stranger in a strange town. He did not even know the name of the town. Bewildered, self-conscious, ill at ease, he drifted with the crowd. Past stores and barber shop, past the eating places, and into a crowded saloon and gambling place.

Nobody was paying him any attention. He found himself at the long bar.

"What'll it be?" asked an overworked man in white jacket and apron.

"Sody pop," said the boy embarrassedly.

"Beer or whiskey, kid. Name it. This ain't any soda fountain."

"Beer, then."

He peeled a twenty-dollar bill from the roll given him by Uncle Jim Taylor.

"Make mine a whiskey," said a man, brushing Bart's elbow. The boy looked at the man, recognizing him as one of the men he had seen at Brown's Park. The man was looking at him sharply.

"I'll buy the next one, button. This is on you."

"If I wasn't good enough to camp with you, then I don't reckon I'm good enough to drink at the bar with ya. If ya need a drink, buy one."

"So that's the way of it, is it, kid? Tough talk for a young 'un. You better be learnin' some manners. I've a good mind to slap some learnin' into you."

"I don't think," said Bart, his face a little

white, "that you're man enough for the job."

The man laughed harshly and struck at the boy. A swift, although clumsy, swing that grazed Bart's cheek. Now Bart's fists were flying like flails. Unscienced, but quick and hard and well-timed were those fists. Next Bart tripped the man and went into a clinch. His knotted fists tore in the older man's stomach. Bart fought like a wild animal, fierce, punishing, and without mercy. It was Bart's first fight. His one and only thought was to beat this man to a bloody pulp, to kill him. Blinded by rage, he fought against the man who fought back. They were on the floor now, gouging, biting, clawing, hitting. Bart tore at the bleeding face. His hands gripped the man's throat, and he clamped down hard. He was pounding the fellow's head against the floor.

Now strong hands were pulling at him. Bart fought them blindly. Blood filled his eyes and mouth. He shook the man's throat, cursing him. They were prying Bart away from the now unconscious man. The bartender was throwing a pail of cold water in his face. There was a crowd gaping at the blood-smeared boy when he began to see clearly through the red haze that had marred his vision. They were working over the man on the floor. Somebody was slapping Bart's back.

"A fightin' fool . . . just a kid, but he had taken that big cuss to a bad cleanin'. And if the big son-of-a-bitch is dead, then a good riddance, and Mike Driscoll's roll is behind the lad. The big feller started it, so I hear. The lad done no more than right. Give the bye a nip o' somethin', Terrence. And git a towel an' a bit of a sponge. And it's Mike Driscoll's bank roll that says the lad has the makin's of a champ, no less. Wit' some trainin', he'd be a wonder. And it's Mike Driscoll who has seen 'em all, as knows a pair o' dukes when he sees 'em. 'Tis the heart o' the bye that makes or breaks him. Terrence, are ye nailed to the floor? A nip for the bye. And a nip o' the same fer me. Then I'm takin' the lad under me own personal wing, and may bad luck befall the bully as annoys us in any way, shape, or manner. And take the bleedin' bully's form outside. If he dies, I'll pay fer the funeral. If he don't die, run him out o' the camp. But don't be lettin' the likes o' such be dirtyin' up me clean floor. Terrence, see that there's some fresh sawdust sprinkled here. Someone wit' money might slip an' break a bone, here on a floor runnin' wit' gore. And now, me lad, what might be the name an' what are ye usin' fer money at the moment?"

"My name is Bart."

"Bart, is it? And the last name is what?"

"Just Bart, sir."

"Oho, an' so it is, me bye. 'Tis a good name, though a bit abrupt. A broth of a bye, ye are. And hungry, no doubt. And may I ask, Terrence, what's the reason of the grin that makes ye look more silly than ever?"

"He's not busted, Mike. He cracked a twenty of a roll that'd choke a cow."

"So the wind blows that way? Terry, the bye is a stranger. Bart, lad, give Terrence the bank roll to put away safe. 'Twill be returned intact to ye, laddie. And now we'll be seein' a few stores an' such. Is it yer first trip here, Barty?"

"Yes, sir." Bart warmed to the big, red-necked Irishman with bushy white hair, a pair of fists like hams, and eyes as blue as the summer sea. A man whose bluff manner hid a heart as full of sentiment as that of a child.

"Terrence, put away the bye's money. 'Tis a meal he needs, and someone to look after him. Ye'll need no money, Barty, while Mike Driscoll has ye in tow. What's yer wishes?"

"A pair of boots," said Bart, "and a haircut, and some clean clothes. But that ain't my money, it's Uncle Jim Taylor's."

"Say that once more. Jim Taylor? Ye know Uncle Jimmy?"

"Yes, sir."

"And did ye ever meet a red-headed idiot called Plunkett?"

"Yes, sir. Hank Plunkett."

"Where, lad, where?"

"In Montana. I was. . . ."

"*Shhhhhh.* Terrence, change the money for the bye, ye understand? 'Tis Uncle Jimmy's bank roll." He took Bart by the arm and escorted the boy down the street.

"You know Uncle Jim Taylor, sir?"

"As well as I know meself, lad. Ye stopped at Brown's Park?"

Bart told Mike Driscoll of his cold reception at Brown's Park.

"A man wit' black eyes, was he? Wit' maybe a scar on the left side av his face? Yes? Then, Bart, lad, ye've done Mike Driscoll a favor this night. And the bully ye licked was wan o' the crowd, was 'e? Faith, and ye put Mike Driscoll in debt to ye, lad. Because whin that black-eyed divil comes here, he comes to do Mike Driscoll no favors. Have ye word from Uncle Jimmy?"

"No, sir. I'm afraid that he's . . . that he's dead."

"Bet wance more, Barty. That old rooster is tough. If Uncle Jimmy Taylor was dead, 'tis Mike Driscoll would be hearin' of it by the rustlin' of the leaves, ye understand. Come now, Barty, and we'll be takin' in the town. Meanwhile, Terrence will be changin' your money into smaller and safer currency." He winked slyly at the boy, who wondered just what the big Irishman meant.

Then began a tour of the town. Mike Driscoll seemed to know every person in town. They hailed him with boisterous good humor. Fate had marked this night for high adventure. Before sunrise, Bart was destined to see strange things and obtain knowledge that would further bewilder his boy's brain.

VIII

"Off Again"

Bathed, shaved, his hair trimmed, arrayed in new clothes from skin outward, and from hat to boots, Bart felt like a real man. Big Mike Driscoll had insisted on paying for it all, and also footing the bill for a grand supper. The first meal Bart had ever eaten in a restaurant. And while the hour was between midnight and dawn, the town was wide awake. Mike Driscoll led the boy back to his saloon and into a private office. They had just sat down in there, when a commotion started out in the barroom. Mike Driscoll stepped from his office. A shot ripped past his head, the leaden slug burying itself in the door casing. Half a dozen masked men stood at the front and rear doors, covering the crowd with blue-barreled guns. The crowd, men and women, stood with arms held high.

Now Mike Driscoll stepped back into

the office. He jerked a big six-shooter from its holster. The next minute the big saloon man was trading shots with the masked men. The bartender, Terrence, was also shooting. A tall man, with a drooping gray mustache, was crouched behind a heavy pool table, thumbing the hammer of his .45.

Then the firing ceased. Mike Driscoll stepped from his office, an ugly gash across his cheek, his blue eyes slitted and hard. Bart, his own gun in his hand, followed the big man. Mike Driscoll bent over a man who lay in a grotesque, motionless heap there by the door. Mike's big hand tore away the black silk handkerchief that had been the man's mask. There was a bullet hole between the man's staring, glazing eyes. Bart recognized the dead man as the black-eyed man at Brown's Park. Now Mike Driscoll turned to the tall man with the mustache. He smiled grimly.

"Know him, Sheriff? Would ye be recognizin' the mug of him?"

The sheriff nodded. "Bill Bolin. You got him dead center, Mike. I think I might 'a' hit one of 'em, but they got away. Terrence winged another. They didn't have much luck."

"Thanks to this lad here, Sheriff, and

they did not. The bye tipped me off that Bill Bolin was camped at Brown's Park wit' some men. Knowin' Bolin hated me, an' puttin' two and twice togither, I told Terrence to be on the watch fer a stick-up, and I sent ye word that ye might be needed in here before mornin'. Aye, it was the Barty lad as saved me bank roll, for I was gittin' careless, Sheriff."

The sheriff was looking hard at Bart. "What's the name, young feller?"

"Barty Jones," put in Mike Driscoll quickly, "and a fine broth of a bye he is. Workin' these past six months at the Horsehead Ranch, jinglin' the remuda. In town fer a good time. Have a drink wit' me, Sheriff, while the swamper cleans up the mess, an' they take Bill Bolin's carcass outta me sight. Fresh sawdust, as the poet says, covers a multitude of sins."

He piloted the sheriff toward the bar. As he passed Bart, the saloon man nudged the boy's ribs and beckoned toward the rear door. Bart felt the piercing scrutiny of the sheriff's keen eyes. Then the law officer and the big saloonkeeper marched to the bar.

Mike Driscoll had glibly lied about Bart. The boy stood out in the dark alleyway behind the saloon and gambling house and dance hall combined. He had felt the swift suspicion of the tall sheriff's eyes. He wondered if old Haddock had sent a description of him this far? Or was it that this eagle-eyed law officer made a habit of scrutinizing and questioning every stranger?

From outside in the darkness that precedes dawn, Bart stood flattened against some empty beer cases and barrels. He knew that Mike Driscoll wanted him to stay hidden until the law went out and down the street to care for the dead Bill Bolin.

Bill Bolin. A dread name along the outlaw trail. The name of a man not to be trusted by his own kind. An outlaw who had been known to talk too much. Bart had heard of Bill Bolin. Other men along that grim and sinister trail spoke of Bill Bolin with contempt and a little fear. For Bill Bolin had borne the reputation of being a deadly killer, a cold-blooded man with a gun who was wont to fight unfairly. Bart had heard Bill Bolin called many hard names by Uncle Jim Taylor. That explained Bart's cold reception at Brown's Park.

There was the odor of stale beer and whiskey there in the dark alley, that was piled with empty casks and kegs and barrels. From inside came the confused jumble of noises. The music of the tin-pan piano that needed tuning. A drunken man lurched out of the back door and headed a wavering, unsteady course for somewhere.

For what seemed a long time the boy crouched there in the darkness. Then the rear door opened, and Mike Driscoll's big frame stood outlined against the light within.

"Are ye there, Barty?"

The boy moved out of the shadow, and Mike Driscoll hustled him inside and into the office. There was a worried look on the face of the big saloon man.

"It ain't what ye might call safe fer ye here, lad. Sheriff Pat Bartlett has suspicions. He has ye connected with a lad as run off from some ranch in Montana. A man named Haddock has a big reward posted fer the return of this lad who, strange to say, goes by the name of Bart. This Haddock is the guardeen of this bye, and wants him fetched home. So puttin' twice and two togither, I'm thinkin' ye better be slidin' out before daylight. Terrence has the money all changed into smaller bills. He'll pass the other money in his own fashion, safe an' easy. So, me bye, if the hand o' the law folds down on ye, ye'll have no evidence on yer person as might be injurious an' damagin'."

"What do you mean?" asked Bart.

"Faith now, an' 'tis smart ye are. Sayin' no word, even to Mike Driscoll, as has passed many a hundred dollars of stolen bills, numbered an' posted and as dangerous to handle as so much dynamite. Now best get ye gone, Barty, before Sheriff Pat Bartlett gits to smellin' around. Head fer the Cross K Ranch, and tell whoever is there that Mike Driscoll sent ye. Tell thim that ye're out of bakin' powder. Good luck to ye, lad. And Uncle Jim Taylor will be showin' up wan of these fine evenin's, bright as a whistle. Now, so long, Barty. Good luck to ye."

The boy's hand was gripped in Mike Driscoll's huge fist. Then he was given a roll of banknotes and ushered out the back door.

Bart made his way to the barn. He was about to go inside when voices at the corral arrested his attention. He instantly recognized the voice of the tall sheriff.

"His horse must be here in the corral or in the barn, Bill. He's a tall, black-haired kid. New clothes. Take him alive. He's come down the trail with old Uncle Jim Taylor. He was mixed up with Hank

Plunkett. They're probably usin' the button to pass some uh that money from the U.P. train hold-up. Old Uncle Jim Taylor got a wad of that dough. They nabbed him in Wyoming, but the slippery old cuss got away. Plunkett's hid out somewheres. Bill Bolin did a little talking the other day to one uh our men that was there at Brown's Park, playin' off as a bad 'un. Nab this kid an' he'll talk, Bill. Lay here at the barn. I'm goin' back tuh Driscoll's an' look aroun'. There's a reward on the button, too. His guardeen in Montana has a reward uh one thousand dollars posted. Must think a lot of the boy. I'll see you later."

Bart slid into the barn. He got his carbine, and shoved it into the saddle scabbard. Then he untied his dun-colored horse and mounted the animal there in the stall.

A man carrying a lantern was just coming into the barn. Bart saw the gun in the man's hand, saw the gleam of a badge pinned to the deputy's vest. Bart jabbed the horse with the spurs. The stout dun horse lunged forward. Bart knocked the man's lantern out of his hand with a swift blow as the horse all but ran down the startled deputy. The man staggered back, blinded by the sudden assault. In the darkness, Bart raced out the open door, swung down the dusty street, and was gone in the night.

IX

"Saved"

Alone once more under the stars, safe from pursuit, Bart slacked the pace of the dun horse. It was getting toward daylight, and Bart wanted to reach his well-hidden camp before he met anyone along the trail.

Inside, he felt sick. If he were to believe what Mike Driscoll inferred, and what the tall sheriff said, then Hank Plunkett and Uncle Jim had been using him as a tool, a dupe, to pass stolen money. It hurt everything in his boy's heart to think that Hank and Uncle Jim would so use him. Then, had their talks of God and honesty been plain lies? Had they been secretly laughing at him because he believed in them? What was a boy to believe if those two men had not been honest with him?

Bart had surmised that Hank Plunkett and Uncle Jim Taylor were not on the best of terms with the law, but he had labeled their wrongdoings as something big, something that was somehow justified in the eyes of God. But if they had used a gullible boy to pass their bad money, then what other petty crimes had they committed?

Bart had a mind to go back to town and talk to the sheriff. But he felt that was being disloyal to Hank Plunkett and Uncle Jim and big Mike Driscoll. Even if they had done him a scurvy trick, yet he could be a man and fight this out in a man's way.

In an agony of disillusionment and uncertainty, Bart rode for his camp in the hills. He felt that he could never again trust the word of any man.

He hoped that nobody had found his camp. He made up his mind to move right after breakfast. Keeping to the untraveled trails, he would head southward. He would avoid all men. He would camp alone. And he would never again take any man's word for anything.

Bitterness filled his heart. He felt actually sick inside. Why had Uncle Jim and Hank Plunkett used those slick lies? Why hadn't they come out in the open and told him they were part of a crew of train robbers? They might have trusted him that far. But, no, they'd made a fool out of him, fed him a lot of smooth talk about telling the truth, and stringing his bets with God Almighty. Was that any way to treat a boy?

Still, he hadn't any real proof. It was hard to believe wrong of the good-natured, rusty-haired Hank Plunkett. It was hard to accuse Uncle Jim of being no better than a smooth liar. Nope, he'd not think badly of them till he'd had the chance to ask them straight out. That was the way. Uncle Jim had preached about the loyalty of friends. To think badly of Hank and Uncle Jim was doing them wrong. But, gosh, things looked mighty bad. They did, for a fact.

Now he neared his camp in the first dim light of dawn. The furry ears of the dun-colored horse twitched. The handsome head with its black mane and foretop was at attention. The flinty black hoofs picked their way daintily along the dim trail. Bart slid his six-shooter free of its holster. He knew that someone had found his camp and was there waiting for him.

"They ain't takin' me back," he gritted. "They ain't takin' me."

He leaned forward in his stirrups, his gun ready. Now he caught the odor of campfire smoke. Saw the blaze through the trees. His heart pounded against his ribs. Perhaps it was Uncle Jim or Hank Plunkett. All anger or bitterness toward them vanished. It would be almighty good to see either of them. No enemy would be lighting a fire. Must be a friend. Now, as he rode into the little clearing, he saw a man squatted there beside the fire, a skillet in his hand. The man looked cross one shoulder as the boy approached. Bart had never before seen the man.

Black stubble covered the lower part of the man's face. Against this blackness and the deeply tanned cheeks above, white teeth gleamed, and a pair of black eyes looked from under straight black brows. A saddle gun lay alongside the man's right boot heel, and Bart noticed that the skillet was in the fellow's left hand. His right hand was hidden.

"I've taken the liberty of helping myself here at your camp," the man said. "I was hungry. Haven't seen food for three days. I'd gotten a little desperate, you see. I've money to pay for what I eat."

The white teeth showed in a smile, but Bart felt the man's eyes coldly studying him. The boy put away his gun and dismounted there by the fire.

"You're plumb welcome to what's here. I don't ask pay. There ain't much here to eat. Bread and meat and coffee."

"Bread and meat and coffee look good

to a starving man."

The man's eyes were hollow and blood-shot. There was a strained, bitter look about his mouth. A handsome man, gray at the temples. His clothes had once been the best that money could buy. The beaver hat and glove-fitting boots had been things of beauty. But they were soiled and torn now.

"Directly I unsaddle, sir, I'll git the breakfast. You kin lie down on my blankets. If ya'd care for a drink of likker, there's a jug hid under them bushes. I'll do the cookin' while you git some rest. I'll wake ya if I hear anybody comin'."

"Are you all alone here at this camp, boy?"

"Plumb alone."

The man's hard black eyes stared into Bart's. He nodded to himself and smiled.

"I reckon I can trust you, boy. That is, so far as any man can put trust in any other man. And a nip of whiskey won't harm a bit. You are a generous host, young man."

The man's voice was soft of tone, Southern in accent, by far the most pleasant voice Bart had ever heard. From the man's manner of speaking, Bart judged him to be a gentleman of some education. Yet he did not trust the man. His eyes, when he studied the boy, were cold, deadly. He carried two Colt guns with white ivory handles. One under each armpit in a holster that fastened in a sort of harness. His carbine was a beautiful weapon with scrollwork on the metal and a stock of black walnut. The man, now noticing the look of admiration in the boy's eyes, smiled.

"Guns are my great love. A weapon like this is to me a thing of rare beauty. Steel of the finest, beautiful wood. Craftsmanship, art in the finishing of such a gun. Perfectly balanced, light, effective. A man who made a bad shot with such a weapon should deserve hanging. Now, young sir, I will warm my emptiness with a drink of your liquor. I drink to your health and happiness."

Behind his words Bart sensed a mockery, a strange, terrible hardness and bitterness.

"Is your horse taken care of?"

The man nodded and smiled. "Otherwise, my young friend, I could not drink or eat."

He returned to the fire, where Bart now prepared breakfast. The drink seemed to put new strength into the man.

"Considerable of an outfit for a lad traveling alone."

"My pardner is ketchin' up with me somewhere along the trail. He had to stay behind . . . on business."

"You just came from town, I'd judge by your new clothes. You are acquainted in town?"

"No, sir."

"There were some men camped at Brown's Park. I saw their sign there. I wonder if you know who they were?"

"One of the men was named Bill Bolin."

"Bill Bolin." The man's eyes narrowed and he ran the palm of his hand across his gun. "I wonder if you know where I could cut the sign of this man, Bill Bolin?" He was looking at Bart with a smile that made the boy suddenly shiver.

"Bill Bolin is dead. He got killed last night."

"Hah! And what might be the name of that kind benefactor to mankind who rid the earth of Black Bill Bolin?"

"A big feller named Mike Driscoll killed him."

"Mike Driscoll! A big man with blue eyes and a brogue as thick as the fog off the Irish coast? There would be another good Irishman with him, Terrence Fogarty?"

"Yes, sir."

"And so good old Mike Driscoll did the job. This man Bolin was a bad lot. He's been cheating the gallows for years. A man without one single saving grace." The man laughed shortly. It was a brittle, unpleasant laugh. "I reckon that's what men say of Lee Waldron," he continued.

"I never run acrost any Lee Waldron."

"You have the doubtful honor of being Lee Waldron's host this morning."

"Oh." Into the boy's mind came the memory of the day when Hank Plunkett had asked him if he had ever run across a Texas cowboy named Lee Waldron or Lee Witten or Lee Watson. Then this was the man who Hank sought. Uncle Jim had told Bart that it was to locate this same Lee Waldron that Hank had risked his life by returning to the Figure 8 range.

It was on the tip of the boy's tongue to ask Waldron if he was a friend of Hank Plunkett's. Then he recalled Hank's advice. Keep a closed mouth always. To ask such a question might kick up some kind of ruckus.

Uncle Jim Taylor had given the boy little information concerning Lee Waldron, except that he might be using one of several names, and that certain pride made the man hold to the name of Lee, because that had been the name of the South's great hero of the Civil War. Uncle Jim had told Bart that Lee Waldron was a killer. But whether he was friend or enemy, Uncle Jim had never said. Bart had never asked.

Now the breakfast was cooked, and they ate in silence. Bart hoped the man would saddle up and pull out. But, instead, Lee Waldron sat there, smoking.

"That breakfast hit the right spot," he told Bart. "And it's made me sleepy. I'm going to trust you, boy. If you hear anyone coming, call me. Or if they get here before you have a chance to call out, tell them that you are alone. If you tip them off that I'm hidden near here, I'll have to kill you. And I'd hate to add to the many sins already chalked against me that I have killed a boy who fed me."

He picked up his carbine, smiled that unpleasant smile, then stalked away. Bart noticed the quick, panther-like step of the man, and how smoothly and silently he moved. Men who are being hunted must acquire the silent habits of other hunted things.

No use trying to move camp now. He'd wait until his uninvited guest had gone, then he'd pack up and move on southward toward New Mexico.

Bart felt drowsy. He had been up all night and was dog-tired. He wanted to crawl off into the brush and sleep, but he was afraid that Lee Waldron would be watching, and would mistake his movements as meaning some kind of treachery, so he sat with his back against a tree and dozed.

How long he was asleep he did not know. He came awake with a jerk. His jaw sagged open. There, standing facing him, were three men. One of them he had little difficulty in recognizing. It was the man with whom he had fought in Mike Driscoll's saloon. There was an ugly leer on the man's swollen, discolored face that bore the marks of his beating. The man's gun covered Bart.

"Sighted your smoke, you young coyote. Thought we'd drop around and pay you a leetle visit. It was you what tipped off Driscoll that we was camped at Brown's Park. You rode in there to squeal, you little, sneakin' coyote. And now Bill Bolin an' another good man is dead on your account. Be sayin' your leetle prayers, kid."

The other two men nodded. "Fix the dirty little squealer so's he can't squawk no more. Only fer him we'd have our pockets filled with Driscoll's dough. Knock his head off with your gun barrel, Pete. Shootin' makes noise that'll bring that sheriff an' his posse in on top uh us. Club him er knife him one."

Bart, upon waking, had jerked to his feet. Too late he remembered he had laid his six-shooter on the ground. Now he stood without a gun. The man, Pete, advanced cautiously, his gun in one hand, a hunting knife in the other. His swollen face spread in a snarling, leering grin. His discolored, puffed eyes glittered. The man was bent on murder.

Bart braced himself, determined to go out fighting. He planned to drop to his knees when the man rushed. He could grab his gun and shoot this ugly-looking renegade.

Every muscle tensed. He clamped his jaws. The man kept coming toward him, crouching, grinning, step after step. Bart saw the other two grinning evilly.

Now the man Pete suddenly halted. The grin was wiped from his face. A hoarse cry from one of the others. Behind Bart, a gun roared. The Pete fellow spun like a top, his right arm limp. Two more shots that blended, and the other two men snarled with pain. Their arms were smashed.

Through the echoes of the gunfire came the voice of Lee Waldron. "That will hold you three brave warriors for some time. Boy, get ropes and we'll tie these three skunks up so they'll be all ready for the sheriff when he follows the sound of the shooting. Quick, lad. Time is worth gold."

Lee Waldron took the pack ropes from Bart. "Kill them if they try to run away, boy. I can tie faster than you."

Swiftly, deftly Waldron tied the three wounded men. Then he called to Bart.

"You can turn 'em over to the sheriff. There'll be a reward. I'm glad I was given the opportunity to repay you for your hospitality. *Adiós,* boy."

But Bart was also moving. "I don't want the sheriff to ketch me, either."

"No? Well, well, starting the game young, aren't you, boy? Well, if you don't care about seeing the law, come with me. We'll leave Pat Bartlett a cold sign to follow."

Saddles cinched. Guns ready. Bart grabbed a cotton sack filled with jerky. Lee Waldron lifted the jug.

"In case the sheriff is delayed, you three brave knights of the sewer will die from loss of blood. It will save the state the expense of boarding you till you stretch rope. Give Sheriff Pat Bartlett the kind regards of Lee Waldron."

They rode away. Bart shuddered at Waldron's refusal to tie up the hurts of the three outlaws. His eyes questioned.

"Waste our golden moments on three

such animals?" Waldron said with a sneer. "Hardly. Come on."

They had ridden some distance before the boy found words to thank this man whose swift guns had saved his life.

"All in a day's span, boy. I heard their voices. By the way, now that fate seems to have made us companions for a few miles, what do I call you?"

"Bart. Just Bart. I don't know my last name."

"Bart? That would be an abbreviation of Bartholomew, perhaps. Or Bartley or Bartlett . . . or perhaps Barton. Where is your home range, boy?"

"Montana."

"Traveling south?"

Bart pointed to the grulla mule, the blue roan, and the G Dot pinto. "Grulla was leadin' me to'rds New Mexico. Now they're follerin' us, so I put the hackamores on the grulla mule and the horses, and led 'em. Sorry I had tuh leave Uncle Jim's stuff behind."

"Who is Uncle Jim?"

"Uncle Jim Taylor, my pardner."

Lee Waldron pulled up with a jerk. "Where is Uncle Jim Taylor?"

"I lost him back on the trail."

"There was a man with him. A red-headed cowboy named Plunkett?"

"Hank Plunkett stayed in Montana, so far as I know."

"Did you ever hear Plunkett speak my name?"

"Yes. He asked me once if I had ever run across a man named Lee Waldron. That was all."

"Hank Plunkett is not in Montana. I hope to locate him in Arizona. He's as hard to put a finger on as a Mexican flea. So you were with Plunkett and Uncle Jim Taylor, were you? Odd they'd be dragging a lad like you along. They're playing a dangerous game. No game for a youngster to be mixed in. I can't understand how they picked you up, or why. No belittling your manliness, son, but a boy your age should not be traveling the outlaw trail. It's a bad trail for any lad. Bad company. Bad influence. What have you done, Bart, that you need to be traveling in the unsavory company of Hank Plunkett, Uncle Jim Taylor, and Lee Waldron? Did you kill anybody? Steal cattle? Rustle horses? Come clean with me, boy, and I'll stake what was once my honor that you'll not regret the confidence. Better wait, though, till we put distance between us. Then we'll pitch camps somewhere and talk it over."

"Mike Driscoll told me to head for the Cross K Ranch."

"Driscoll told you that? Then it's where we'll head for. Know the trail?"

"That grulla mule will find it, I reckon. He knows the trails, day or night."

Now Lee Waldron's laugh held genuine mirth. "Then, Bart, son, what say we turn the grulla mule and his spotted companion loose, and whither the grulla mule leads, we follow. Be it to glory or the gallows. To paradise or purgatory. To music or to the roar of guns. Lead on, Bart. Where you lead, Lee Waldron follows. The wolf led by the lamb. Following a mouse-colored mule toward adventure. The wisdom of an ass."

X

"Hank Appears"

Lee Waldron made an odd companion. Dangerous, always alert, with a bitter tongue and the trained mind of a man who was at once well-read and worldly. Sometimes his voice would soften, and his mood would lose its blackness. He would talk to Bart of many things belonging to a world that the boy despaired of ever glimpsing. A world of art, of beautiful music, tall buildings, theaters, great ocean liners. A world that Lee Waldron spoke of as familiar ground, as if it were to that more genteel world that he belonged. Yet the man knew the country like a book, and could handle a rope or a bronco.

They stayed overnight at the Cross K Ranch, then drifted on, with fresh grub and stout horses. Days and nights of steady travel. Then they pulled into a town in Arizona, where they remained almost a week.

Bart had never quite trusted Lee Waldron. Yet he had no reason to distrust the man who seemed to have no friends along the trail. The men they met seemed to know Lee Waldron and fear him. They watched the handsome renegade with an uneasiness that seemed to amuse the killer. Yet he treated them well enough, was civil, although never talkative, and always held himself apart from them, as if he did not want to thrust his rather unwelcome company upon them.

To Bart alone did the man talk. Then it was in a general manner, as a man might voice his thoughts aloud, knowing that what he said would go no further.

In the Arizona town, Lee Waldron spent his nights playing cards. Now he won, again he lost. Once he went broke, and accepted a $100 loan from Bart. At breakfast time the following morning, he handed Bart $500.

"Half of what I cleaned up last night, Bart. It's yours."

When Bart protested, Lee Waldron explained that it was customary, when staked, to split the winnings two ways. That was part of a gambler's code.

Lee Waldron had purchased new clothes. He was shaved and clothed. He moved about the town with the manner of a man waiting for someone or something to happen. He and Bart had adjoining rooms at a hotel. There was a bath between, and Bart learned to bathe every morning. In his heart he admired this handsome, arrogant man, who sneered at life and seemed to have no fear of anything. Some of the men at the gambling tables seemed to know him. Now and then a cowman nodded to him coldly. But no man ever spoke to Lee Waldron as a friend. Nor did Lee Waldron ever take a drink in the company of any man. All of which caused Bart much wonderment and speculation. Why did other men shun Lee Waldron?

As for Bart, he spent his time idling about the town. It was a town of goodly size, with stores and saloons, a livery barn, a bank, even a newspaper, run by a genial inebriate with bushy white hair and a round paunch. The town marshal was a small-boned, wiry, leathery man with one eye. To the marshal Lee Waldron had spoken of Bart, the first day they came to town.

"I'll vouch for the boy. It don't matter what this man Haddock in Montana has to say about it. Nor do I want you to let the news out that the boy is here with me. The youngster has done no harm. From what he tells me . . . and get it straight that this boy is no liar . . . this old Haddock is a hard-fisted, pinchpenny old hellion. I'm vouching for this boy, regardless of what any notice reads, or what any small-town, two-bit deputy has to say. The boy is on the level."

The one-eyed marshal, a gunman of renown and said to be absolutely fearless as a manhunter, shrugged his lean shoulders. "It'll be up to you, Waldron. You must have a strong reason for hanging onto the kid. You don't do things like that without a reason." The one-eyed marshal spoke with cold dislike for the handsome killer.

"A reason. Perhaps more than one reason. And the reasons might surprise you. It might even be that I like the youngster."

"I never knew you to like anything but a good horse, a fancy gun, or an enemy's corpse. I'm sorry for the boy if he's took to you."

"Save your sympathy," Lee Waldron said with a smile, as he twisted his slender mustache, turned his back on the one-eyed marshal, and walked on.

It was that evening when Bart was washing up for supper that he learned news of Uncle Jim Taylor.

Lee Waldron came in, tossed his hat on the bed, and rolled a slim cigarette.

"Somebody has set you afoot, Bart. The dun-colored horse, the pinto, blue roan, the grulla mule are gone from the corral at the feed barn."

"The mule," said the boy quickly, "wouldn't let any man steal him without makin' a big fight. Same way with the dun horse. Only person besides me that kin git near that mule is Uncle Jim Taylor."

"The barn man said a white-haired old man on a big brown gelding took 'em. When the barn man argued that they belonged to a boy that came to town with Lee Waldron, this old rascal pulled a gun and told the man to make fast tracks. He sent word to me that he was killing me on sight."

"Why?"

"For the same reason a lot of renegades along the outlaw trail would like to take my scalp. Because they hate me. The man who is fast enough and lucky enough to kill me collects a big reward from the outlaws who ride between Mexico and Canada. I think the money is secretly posted with Mike Driscoll. Whenever they make a big haul somewhere, they add some more to the jackpot."

"Why do they hate ya like that?" asked Bart, thinking about Uncle Jim, and wondering why the old fellow had set him afoot.

"They'd tell you that I'm a traitor. That I kill men for the bounty paid for their hides."

Lee Waldron laughed grimly and took from his pocket a certified check. It bore the endorsement of Sheriff Pat Bartlett, and was made payable to Lee Waldron only.

"That was for the three we tied up at your camp below Brown's Park. Fifteen hundred for the three. You'll get your cut when I cash the check, boy."

"I wouldn't handle that kind uh money," said Bart quickly.

A dark flush stained Lee Waldron's handsome face. His black eyes glittered like hot, red sparks. For a moment Bart braced himself against an attack from the man. Then the killer smiled and resumed his cigarette.

"You'd rather spend money that don't belong to you, then? Money gained by robberies. Money that was given you by Uncle Jim Taylor to exchange for money that would not put its owner behind steel bars. The clothes you wear, the grub you eat, the bed you sleep in are paid for by money that does not belong to you. Yet you call reward money, gained by turning over three murderers to the law for hanging, dirty money. So be it. Every man to his own way of thinking. I'm going down now to take this so-called dirty money and bet it on a few hands of poker. If I had your point of view concerning money, I'd go earn a few honest dollars."

Lee Waldron's voice was low-pitched, modulated, and his white teeth showed in a smile, but his black eyes still showed redly. He swung around and left the boy alone in the room.

Bart, torn this way and that by conflicting emotions, sat on the edge of his bed. All appetite for supper was now gone. The pit of his stomach ached as if it held a lump of lead.

Twilight came, but Bart did not make a light. He sat on the edge of the bed in the gathering gloom, trying to puzzle out things. When Hank Plunkett or Uncle Jim had talked to him, it had been easy to believe that those two men were inwardly honest in their dealings. He had trusted them with his youthful confidences. Now this embittered man who called himself a bounty hunter condemned the men he hunted for common thieves who used a gullible boy as a tool. Was Lee Waldron right? Uncle Jim Taylor had given him the money. But he had said nothing to Bart about getting it exchanged. He had simply handed Bart the money and told him to keep it in case he, Uncle Jim, did not show up at camp.

"It's yours. Spend 'er as you like."

"I'll pay 'er all back to him," Bart had said through clenched teeth. "Every last cent. I don't want any man's money. I'll go git me a job and work honest at it."

He heard the door creak, there in the deep gloom of the hotel room. Bart gripped his gun and peered into the uncertain light.

"Ya there, Bart?"

"Hank!" gasped the boy, jumping to his feet. "Hank Plunkett!"

"It's me and none other, boy." Bart heard him lock the door. The boy struck a match, but Hank's hand quickly put out the flame.

"No lights, boy. Not unless you want me shot. I want a few words with you, Bart. They bin a-tellin' me some hard tales about you. Is it true that you've throwed in with Lee Waldron?"

"I came here with him from over near

Brown's Park. But I'm quittin' him to-night. They're hirin' cowboys, and I'm goin' to git me a job. I got Uncle Jim's money here. It's all here. I got aplenty that Lee Waldron won fer me in a card game. Enough to buy me a good outfit and a horse. I'm goin' to work."

"Glad tuh hear it, boy. That's the ticket. I reckon mebbeso Lee Waldron told you thet you was free tuh go, now he'd made use of you and got what he wanted outta you."

"Lee Waldron never made use uh me, Hank."

"No? If he was here, I'd make the big, black-eyed snake tell you a heap different. He used you tuh git Uncle Jim Taylor and me here. We're here, but it just might be tuh Lee Waldron's sorrow that we come when the word came up the trail that you'd told Waldron you was tradin' bad money for good. Ya told him that, Bart?" Hank's voice questioned him.

"No, sir. I did not. If he said that, he lied. I didn't know I had stolen money till Mike Driscoll said so, and a sheriff and a deputy was talkin' about it in that Colorado town where Bill Bolin got killed. I never told any man I had traded stolen money fer good money."

"So I told Uncle Jim," said Hank

234

Plunkett. "When word come up the trail that they had you here in jail, I come on down quick as I could. So did Uncle Jim. But when they claimed you'd talked like that in the jail, I figured they lied and was settin' a trap fer me 'n' Uncle Jim. So we lay low. I find out you're livin' here at the hotel with Lee Waldron, and that, while the town marshal knows ol' Haddock wants you, he's a-lettin' you run plumb loose. Which I tell Uncle Jim that the whole thing smells bad, but before we take any man's word that you are workin' in with that scalp hunter to ketch us, I'll have tuh hear it from you, personal. Lee Waldron's bin usin' you."

"The same as you and Uncle Jim used me to pass that bad money."

Hank whistled softly. Then he chuckled, and stepped to the dark window. For a minute he stood there, looking down on the lighted street. Now he turned from the window and stepped softly to the locked door. He crouched there in the darkness, listening. Then he came back to where Bart stood in the center of the room.

"Somebody out in the hall, a-listenin'. Some fellers down on the street below that don't look so good. I reckon Uncle Jim was right when he said I was a plumb fool tuh risk comin' up here. That other door leads tuh the bathroom, no? Lee Waldron's room beyond. Fellers in the hall. A thirty-foot drop from the window tuh the ground. Lee Waldron's got his trap all baited an' set, ain't he? Got his fancy guns all oiled, I bet."

"What have you done, Hank, that they want you so bad?"

"The warrant reads train robbery an' murder, boy. Better you git into that closet. Lay on the floor. It'll be over in less than two minutes after the play starts. You lay low an' don't do no shootin'. Sorry I ain't got time fer a tune on the harmonica. Mebbeso next time our trails cross I'll git time to play ya a few new 'uns. Into the closet with you, boy." Hank's strong hands gripped Bart's shoulders. "In ya go, Bart, boy."

But Bart was of another mind. He squirmed free and faced the red-haired outlaw.

"We made a gitaway once before, Hank. Take me with you."

"Not this trip. This is gonna be tight an' fast. I'll locate you someday. So long. In you go." This time he pushed the boy into the closet roughly, turned the key in the lock. Bart was a prisoner in the clothes closet.

Now came the crash of a door being smashed in. Shouts, shots. The sharp tinkle of shattered glass. The room was filled with men. There was a lot of shooting. Bart lay there in the closet on the floor, helpless.

"Outside!" shouted the town marshal's voice. "He jumped out the window, men! Got away!"

XI

"Wounded"

Bart lunged against the door of the closet, and pounded on it with his gun. Some man unlocked the door. A lamp had been lighted, for the old hotel was not wired for electricity. Three men stood there with guns in their hands. An unfriendly-looking trio. Bart faced them without flinching.

"Where's Hank Plunkett?" he asked.

"Got away. But Lee Waldron's a-follerin' him. Waldron will fetch him back."

"If he does, he'll fetch him back dead," gritted Bart. "Lemme outta this room."

"Not so fast." A young man not much older than Bart leered. "Our orders says tuh hold you, see?"

"Yeah?" Bart's gun barrel clipped him across the ear. Grabbing the reeling man, Bart used him as a shield. His gun covered the other two who, like their companion, were recruited from the pool hall and saloons to make up the posse. Bart's eyes were blazing. His whole body tingled with the thrill of it.

"Drop your guns, you snakes, or I'll commence on you!"

They obeyed sullenly. Something about this lean, bronzed cowboy spelled danger to them. They dared not disobey. Dared not do anything but stand there helplessly, unarmed, as Bart herded them into the closet and locked the door.

Bart ran into the hallway and down the narrow back stairs. It was dark there on the stairs. A man blocked his way. A gun cracked, and the boy felt the deadly breath of a bullet past his cheek. He upset the man, pounding at the fellow with the barrel of his .45. Then he gained the back door, slid into the shadows of the alleyway, swung up on the first horse he came to, and rode into the night, his horse on a dead run.

Out of the alleyway and onto the main street he went, lying low along the neck of his stolen horse, with shots from windows and doorways, and bullets snarling around him. Then out of town and into the mesquite country beyond, he headed for whatever the night might hold under the stars.

The thrill of high adventure gripped

him, intoxicating his senses like strong wine. He felt like shouting, like yelling at the top of his voice. He had found courage in an hour of danger. He was a man. From now on he would play a man's part, fill a man's place, fight a man's fight.

On and on. Luck had favored him with a great horse. Ahead, the star-spotted night that was filled with danger that he could face without flinching.

Bart laughed through set teeth. He was wishing he could meet old Haddock and make that cruel-hearted old devil cringe, even as Haddock had made a spindle-shanked, browbeaten boy quiver under the rawhide quirt.

"I'll go back," he told the stars, "someday. I'll take the quirt away from that ol' cuss an' lick him till he hollers fer mercy."

He rode along an unknown trail, and twice went off the trail to avoid meeting groups of riders returning to town.

Bart remembered hearing of some rough hills to the eastward. For these hills, taking his bearing from the stars, Bart now rode. He wondered what had become of Hank Plunkett and Lee Waldron. Had they fought it out? And what part had Uncle Jim Taylor played in that daring and spectacular getaway Hank Plunkett had made? He hoped that someday he would again find Hank and Uncle Jim. He wanted Uncle Jim to know that he had no voluntary part in Lee Waldron's trap setting. Hank's voice with its familiar, careless jocularity had stirred the boy's liking for the red-haired man. Yet, by Hank's own confession, he was wanted for train robbery and murder. White-haired, kindly, nature-loving, Scripture-reading Uncle Jim. It was hard to think of Uncle Jim as being anything but trustworthy under any conditions.

Not so, Lee Waldron. If Lee Waldron had set that trap, then Lee Waldron was all that men said of him. He was a skunk, a man who used underhanded ways to trap the men who he killed for the price on their heads. A tricky, sneaking, cowardly bounty hunter. No wonder all men hated him, shunned him, stayed aloof from him. Still, recalling some of the hours he had spent beside lonely campfires, when Bart remembered the softer moods of the killer, he could find more pity than hatred for Lee Waldron.

Life was giving Bart some queer companions. Fate was dealing him cards from a marked deck. In his pocket was money that belonged to Uncle Jim. He'd forgotten to give it to Hank. A twist of luck was making an innocent youth into a hunted animal. Bart had hurt no man, had broken no laws, and yet he rode with a price on his head. He had come from Montana to Arizona along the outlaw trail, in the company of outlaws and killers. Life back at the Figure 8, the beatings he had suffered, the hunger and wet and cold winters, the cast-off clothes old Haddock had thrown at him, the heavy chores, the agony of sleeplessness and tasks far beyond his strength, all those things seemed but a partly forgotten nightmare.

Suddenly, through his dreaming, his musing, broke the harsh challenge of a man.

"*¿Quién es?* Who's ridin'? Reach for the stars, you ramblin' son!"

Before Bart could rein up, before he could obey the command, before he could summon his wool-gathering wits, a shot ripped out of the brush. A thudding, burning sensation was in the boy's shoulder. Now he dug his spurs deeply, jerking his gun. Two men were shooting at him. Another bullet reached Bart, ripping open his thigh. He kept shooting back over his shoulder. Now his running horse was carrying him into the night. He rode with clamped teeth, fighting the pain, the nausea that swept over him, and, as he rode, he reloaded his six-shooter.

The pain grew steadily worse. He felt dizzy, sick to the point of vomiting, but he did his best to tie up his wounds and hold together his courage and fortitude.

Mile after mile, Bart lost track of time. He let his horse find its own way along the trail. Then, when he knew that he must use desperate measures, he unbuckled the lariat and managed to tie himself into the saddle after a fashion.

He did not hear the voice that hailed him out of the night. He did not feel the hands that took him from the saddle and cared for his wounds. He could not hear Uncle Jim Taylor talking to him as he cared for the wounded boy. Nor the voice of Hank Plunkett.

"We'll have ta git the kid somewheres where he'll get proper care, Hank. You better keep on. There's a cow ranch near here. I'll take Bart there. And heaven have mercy on Lee Waldron er ary other son-of-a-snake that bothers the lad. Ride along, Hank. Leave the boy ta me."

XII

"Nan's Fury"

Bart awoke in bed, between cool, white sheets. There were some pictures on the walls, and the window shade was pulled low, so that the room, with its whitewashed walls, was shadowed and cool. He wondered where he was and how he had gotten there. When he moved, he felt a dull pain in his shoulder and one leg. He was wrapped in tight bandages, and there was the clean odor of disinfectant. Between the bed and the window sat a girl with hair like spun copper, and greenish eyes that now looked at him solemnly. She was the most beautiful girl Bart ever hoped to see.

"How did I git here?" was his first question. The girl rose and came to the edge of the bed. A slender girl in a white dress.

"A friend of yours brought you here to this ranch, then he left. I came here from Tucson to nurse you. I'm Hank Plunkett's kid sister. He's been keeping me there at school."

"Then Hank got away safe?"

"Yes. He's in Mexico, I think, with Uncle Jim Taylor. Uncle Jim was the one who brought you here. The Mexicans who own the place took you in. You'll be up and around before long, so the doctor says. I'm glad I studied nursing now instead of stenography."

"It's shore mighty fine of you to be here with me."

The girl had Hank's smile. "That big brother of mine just naturally loaded me on the train and sent me. I didn't have much to say about it. He got me out of bed in the middle of the night. Told me a friend of his named Bart was at this ranch. I was to pack up and hit the trail for here. Hank's a wild Indian."

Bart was horribly afraid of this girl in white. She was the only girl he had ever met. When she took his pulse and examined his bandages, the boy was more embarrassed than he had ever been in his life. She sensed this, and did her best to make him feel at perfect ease.

It developed that her name was Nan and that she and Hank had no parents living, nor any relatives. Hank had raised Nan since she was six years old. She worshiped him, and told Bart that nobody could make her believe Hank was bad.

"Gee, Bart, if you only knew him as I do. How he was mother and father to me, sending me to a convent school and buying me things that I knew he could not afford. Going without things he needed, to buy me the silly trinkets girls like. Nursing me when I had measles and mumps and other kid ailments. Working all day there at our little ranch on the Pecos. Trying to make a stake for me. And don't let any man ever tell you that Hank Plunkett is a train robber. He never stole anything in his life. There's something behind it all. Hank wouldn't tell me. Said that he didn't want me to lie for him if the law officers questioned me."

Nan was seventeen, but she mothered Bart as if he were a small boy. The Mexican family came in to see the wounded cowboy. They were honest, kind-hearted people. A family of seven youngsters. The mother was a buxom woman with very white teeth and soft, brown eyes. Nan talked to her in fluent Spanish. The children, ranging in age from a ten-month-old baby to a shy-mannered girl of thirteen, worshiped Nan. She gave them toys and clothes that she had bought in town. Candy and cookies.

The medical man was a bluff old country doctor, whose skill in patching up bullet wounds spoke of years of long practice in the cow country. He joked with Bart, jollied Nan, looked at the tongues of all the youngsters, and poked them in the ribs with a blunt thumb.

Bart was well on the way to recovery when he learned that he was under arrest. Nan had known it, of course. And the doctor had known it.

It was Sheriff Pat Bartlett who had ordered Bart's arrest. He had learned of the boy's whereabouts and had sent a deputy down from Colorado with papers and blunt orders to fetch back the boy who was mixed up with Hank Plunkett. The charge against Bart was horse stealing, and Mike Driscoll was the man who had sworn out the warrant.

"But I never stole any horse from Mike Driscoll," Bart told the deputy who came one day with the doctor.

The deputy shrugged his shoulders. "That's something you'll have to settle in court. I got my orders. Better keep your mouth shut till ya git a lawyer. The doctor says it'll be about two weeks before you kin be moved. Your bond was fixed by your friends. I'll be back here for ya in two weeks. So long, Bart."

That was that. Bart wondered what could be Mike Driscoll's game. He got an inkling of it in a few days after the deputy had called. Bart was sitting out on the porch when he saw a rider coming along the trail. He made sure that the .45 was handy under the blanket that lay across his lap. He heard Nan singing inside the house as she cooked chicken broth.

As the rider came nearer, Bart's eyes hardened. The man who was coming was Lee Waldron.

Lee Waldron swung from his saddle, a thin smile on his lips. A handsome, arrogant figure, well-groomed, sinister. He met Bart's scowling eyes with a shrug. He slumped into a chair with a rawhide seat and rolled a thin cigarette of Mexican tobacco.

"I heard you were getting excellent care, or I'd have come sooner."

"Was there any reason for comin' at all?" asked Bart.

"Perhaps not. They tell me that you go back to Colorado to stand trial on a horse-stealing charge."

"What of it?"

"Nothing. I was just making conversation. By the way, the two men who waylaid you won't bother you any more. They'll be doing time for the next twenty-five years. You must have done some neat shooting in the dark, because each of them had a hole in his hide. They were a part of the Bill Bolin crowd. That just about cleans up that pack of coyotes."

"How much did they bring you?" Bart's tone was cold.

The killer smiled. "Five hundred apiece. I've put the money in the bank to your account. You'll be needing money."

"Not that money."

"Suit yourself, Bart. It's there whenever you change your mind. By the way, if you have any means of communicating with Hank Plunkett, I wish you'd let him know that I didn't engineer that deal at the hotel. That fool marshal did that. Double-crossed me. When I go after Hank Plunkett, I don't ask for any help from any man. He should know that."

"You used me as bait to git Hank. You can't lie outta that."

"I'm not trying to, son. I admit it was using you shabbily. But I wanted to meet Hank Plunkett. I planned on meeting him alone, however. The trap they laid was not one of mine. Get that word to Hank Plunkett. Also, get word to him, if you can, that I've seen Mike Driscoll, and that the train-robbery charge and the murder charge against him are dropped. And I suppose you know by now that the money given to you by Uncle Jim Taylor was honest money. Neither Uncle Jim Taylor nor Hank Plunkett had a thing to do with that U.P. train hold-up. Bill Bolin framed that lie. Mike Driscoll sent his best re-gards, Bart."

Bart's mouth twisted somewhat crook-edly. "Sent 'em in the shape of a warrant."

"Quite so. We had to work fast, too."

"We?"

Lee Waldron laughed softly. "Mike and I and Terrence."

"Collecting another bounty?" sneered Bart.

"Call it what you wish, son. But at any rate, it blocked old Haddock's plan to have you arrested and taken back to Montana. You're under arrest for stealing a horse from Mike Driscoll. Doctor's orders are that you can't be moved. In two weeks' time, let's say, you'll be able to ride again . . . in a southerly direction. Let's surmise that you'll be about twenty-four hours ahead of the Colorado deputy. And the man old Haddock is sending down with a warrant to be served in Colorado will be left looking rather foolish. Your bond was only two hundred and fifty dollars, which you can pay off if you ever get a million."

"You mean," said Bart, "that you and Mike Driscoll framed this deal to cheat old Haddock?"

"Something like that, son." Lee Waldron got to his feet.

Bart sat there, stunned by the news. Lee Waldron and Mike Driscoll had saved him from being returned to Montana.

Lee Waldron stood there, smiling down at the boy, his black eyes softening.

"You'll get the news to Hank Plunkett that I didn't know that fool marshal was going to trap him? Send word to Plunkett that when I come after him, I'll come alone. And now, son, *adiós*."

"Hold on!" cried Bart huskily. "I'm plumb in debt to you. You git me to hatin' you, then do somethin' that makes me feel low down. I'm owin' to you, Lee Waldron, and I'll pay my debt. If I bin wrong in judgin' you, then I'm mighty sorry."

"Spoken like a man, Bart. And I thank you for it. I'll be back before you go, unless some quick-triggered gentleman downs me. *Adiós*."

251

As Lee Waldron stepped up on his horse, Nan Plunkett stepped out on the porch. The killer swept off his hat. Nan stood there, staring at him, her face pale. Then she stepped back in the house, appearing a moment later with a shotgun held firmly in her hands.

"Get down off that horse, Lee Waldron!" she called.

"I'm sorry, Nan Plunkett, but I have business that forbids me the pleasure of your charming company."

Reining his horse around, and lifting his hat, Lee Waldron rode away, his horse swinging along the trail at a pacing walk. Nan stood there, trembling a little, her eyes blazing, the shotgun in her hands. Then she turned on Bart, whose right hand now held a six-shooter.

"If Hank Plunkett is your friend," she said fiercely, "call that murderer back here and kill him. Kill him, Bart!"

But Bart sat there dumbly, staring after Lee Waldron, voiceless.

XIII

"Trapped"

"Coward!" Nan's husky voice struck Bart like the sting of old Haddock's rawhide quirt.

His eyes met hers for a moment, then shrank at the contempt for him that he read there, as he stared after Lee Waldron. Something about that straight-backed horseman gave the boy courage. He felt hot inside with resentment toward that red-haired girl. He got to his feet, holding to the rail of the porch for support.

"I never killed a man," he told her. "Whenever I do, I won't shoot him in the back."

"Why didn't you make him come back and face you, then?"

"Because he'd uh just laughed at me, for one thing. For another thing, I have no quarrel with Lee Waldron. I'm plumb in his debt."

"Obligated to that hide hunter? In debt to that murdering snake? Then I'm sorry for you. Speak the name of Lee Waldron to any honest man in Texas, and hear what they say of him. He kills men for the bounty he can get on their dead bodies. Even the horse thieves loathe his name. Right now he came here, hunting sign of Hank, my brother. And you, you who owe your very life to my brother, let Lee Waldron ride away without lifting a gun to stop him. You're afraid of him, I suppose. A lot of men are afraid of him. I wish I had shot him."

"Why didn't you shoot?" asked Bart, his face pale and strained.

"Because, perhaps, I thought you were man enough to handle the job."

Nan turned sharply and went back into the house, her green eyes wet with unshed tears. She went into her own room, and threw herself on the bed, her slim, white-uniformed figure racked by sobs.

Bart, miserable, sick from the girl's accusation and her utter contempt for him, stood there a moment on the porch. Then he walked slowly, limpingly toward the barn. No one was about.

Saddling his horse was rather a slow job, for he had the use of only one arm.

Mounting was a little awkward. Without a backward glance, he rode away from the Mexican ranch.

Perhaps Bart hoped that Nan would come running after him with words that would salve the hurt in his heart. Perhaps he wished for something like that, for he was still hardly more than a boy, with a boy's heart and a boy's way of thinking.

But Nan did not call him. She lay on her bed, sobbing, unaware of the fact that Bart had gone. She told herself how she hated Bart, and that he was a weakling and a coward. Yet she knew that, deep down in her innermost heart, Bart's place there was not the place that a weakling or a coward could ever take. Yet, because, after all, Nan Plunkett was only seventeen and a girl, she would not yet concede that she had been in the wrong. She only knew that Bart had not called Lee Waldron back when she had commanded that he do so.

It was about two hours later when Nan washed her tear-stained face, powdered her nose, and in a fresh uniform took Bart's tray to the boy's room.

The room was empty. She took the tray out to the porch. Bart was not there. Alarmed, she set down the tray and called the Mexican woman. Nobody had seen

Bart ride away. It had been the *siesta* hour when the household slept.

The empty stall and the saddle missing from its peg told the tale. The Mexican who owned the ranch was away with his *vaqueros*, gathering cattle. Nan ran back to the house and changed from her white uniform to riding togs — whipcord breeches, a pair of high-heeled cowboy boots hand-made by the best boot maker in Texas, a flannel shirt, and buckskin jumper. A black Stetson completed her costume, save for a light rifle and a pearl-handled .32 that she carried in a carved-leather holster.

Alarmed, angry, penitent, she set out after the missing Bart. She picked up the tracks of his horse and followed as swiftly as she dared without losing the trail. But, with a two-hour start, she could hardly hope to catch up with him much before dark.

Now she saw tracks of a second horse. Lee Waldron's? Some sheriff's spy who had been watching the ranch, expecting Bart to escape? Fear gripped Nan. Fear for the safety of the wounded cowboy. She was blaming herself for being a hot-tempered, sharp-tongued little wildcat.

The trail turned and twisted, crossing mesa and draws, heading deep barrancas, climbing, dropping again, clinging to the side of brush-covered hills, where hunted men hid. Few honest men ever rode through these rough hills. Now and then strong posses, led by some grim-jawed sheriff, combed the hills for some man they wanted, but few, indeed, were the law officers who rode alone here.

Certainly it was no country for a lone girl to be riding in. These hills held men of every description. Renegades of all colors, who lived like hunted beasts. Men wanted for every crime known. Nan had heard Bart and the Mexican rancher talking about a pack of these human beasts who had been raiding the ranches farther south, killing, stealing, burning.

Then Nan made a disturbing discovery. She had been following the sign of two horses, and now the tracks of but one horse showed. She had been sighted by the second rider, who had hidden along the trail and let her pass. She was trailing Bart alone. This other man was trailing her. It gave her a creepy feeling between her shoulders. She wondered how far behind this man could be. Who was he? What was his game? She realized full well the folly of riding there, unprotected. It was nearing sundown. Too late now to turn back and be out of the rough hills before darkness shut her here in its black jaws.

Her one hope was to catch Bart before darkness came. She'd feel less frightened with Bart near her. She quickened the gait of her horse. The trail rimmed up the side of a cañon, and through a wide saddle. Looking back, she thought she caught sight of a man on horseback. But she could not be sure, for the distance between was half a mile, and it might have been a steer or cow.

She rode through the wide saddle and into a beautiful valley, filled with tall pines. She saw some wild cattle that broke into a run at sight of her. The valley was already in the first gloom of twilight. The birds no longer sang. She felt shut in, trapped. The valley lost its majestic beauty and became a place of danger. Small sounds stirred in the brush. The pines seemed to whisper of hidden dangers.

Then, abruptly, so suddenly that she had no time to think, four roughly garbed, heavily armed men rode out of a side trail and toward her. She saw the glitter of raw steel, saw them spread out as they rode toward her. One of them was a giant Negro, another a half-breed of mongrel blood. They looked ugly enough for any crime.

"Hang it all if it ain't a gal!" The lean-faced man with dirty, tobacco-stained whiskers of sandy color laughed.

"A gal in men's clothes!" added the half-breed.

They had ridden up to her with drawn guns. Now the four of them leered and grinned and eyed her with brutal eyes. Escape was impossible. Nan had pulled her .32, and this seemed to give the men a great deal of amusement.

"If she was tuh shoot a man with that there popgun," scoffed the lean-jawed man, "and a man was tuh find out he'd bin hit, he might git right huffy. Jim," he continued, pointing to the Negro, "I bet she could empty that gun at ya, and them things she's usin' fer bullets would bounce off your black head like hailstones off a slate roof."

"Keep away from me," she said, trying to make her voice sound courageous. "I can shoot, and I will. Let me pass."

"Now, now, young missy, don't git so hasty. Us boys are all real gents. It ain't so often as we git such purty company. We're just jolly, fun-lovin' fellers as leads a lonely life here in the hills, 'count uh our love fer roamin'. Not exactly family men, but we're all fine fellers when ya git tuh know us good. Our clothes might need a leetle patchin' an' pressin', and we could stand barberin' some, but our hearts is the heart uh gold as ya read about. Nary one of us 'u'd harm a hair uh that purty red head. If ya feel like passin' up such company, then we opens the trail fer you. Jim, you an' Pelón pull aside, while the lady rides on. Sorry you won't throw in with four jolly fellers, missy. Let 'er pass!"

The huge Negro and the half-breed pulled their horses off the trail; Nan spurred her horse forward. As she passed, the two grabbed her arms. Her gun barked with futile effort before it was knocked from her hand.

"Now" — the lean-jawed renegade chuckled — "tie 'er arms and we'll git tuh camp."

Nan struggled helplessly against their strength. When she shattered the quiet, pine-clad valley with wild screams, they shoved a gag in her mouth, and the leader slapped her brutally.

"Shut up, you little hellcat."

The big Negro led her horse. They hit a fast trot. The pine forest swallowed them. About half an hour later they reached a cabin in a little clearing. Smoke curled from the stone chimney. A horse grazed at the end of a stake rope. Nan's gag prevented her from giving a startled cry. Because the horse that grazed there on the picket rope was Bart's horse.

XIV

"The Rescuer"

Bart, leaving the Mexican ranch, had headed for the rough hills. He knew that somewhere in these hills he would find Lee Waldron, and he wanted to ask Lee Waldron some questions concerning Hank Plunkett and Uncle Jim Taylor. Determined now to follow this thing through to the finish, he was going to make Lee Waldron explain things.

Mile after mile he followed the trail that led into the rough hills that were the barricade of this side of a spot called Lost Valley. He figured that, sooner or later, Lee Waldron would show up. He would make the killer answer those questions he would ask. He would clear his own debt to Waldron, then feel free to face him as an enemy if the play came up that way. Or, if Lee Waldron was not the snake that Nan Plunkett claimed him to be, he could face her with proof of the killer's honesty. Lee Waldron had made it hard for the boy to hate him. On the other hand, there remained the indisputable fact that all men hated this handsome, sinister killer with his black eyes, his silvering hair, his chilled smile, and his deadly guns. They called Lee Waldron a bounty hunter. Yet Bart knew that the man cared little for money. He gambled it away, threw it away as if he hated it. And he had vaguely hinted that somewhere behind him was a reason for what he did.

Bart had reached the hills, had ridden through the wide saddle, and into Lost Valley. By pure accident, he had found the cabin there in the pines. Weak, hungry, half-sick with pain from the bandaged shoulder that throbbed incessantly, he had staked his horse in the clearing, and had made free use of the cabin that was stocked with grub. Knowing that Lost Valley was the home of cattle rustlers, he had used that right of the man who rides the outlaw trail, and had made himself welcome.

Now, as he started supper, he heard the thud of shod hoofs. He had seen the four men ride up. He had recognized Nan. While the others halted outside, the long-jawed leader, his gun in his hand, stepped into the cabin. Bart, with his blood-stained bandages, his drawn face, his boyish grin, faced the renegade's gun.

"I kinda stumbled on this cabin, mister," he said. "Bein' kinda wore out an' hungry, I taken the chance on bein' throwed out when ya got here. If ya want me to pull out, say so. I got money to pay fer my grub."

Bart looked into a pair of pale, furtive, cunning eyes. The gun in the renegade's hand covered him, but the boy did not flinch. Hidden under that bloodstained bandage around his shoulder was his .45. It was in under his shirt, below his armpit, but where he could get it quickly.

"Ya got money, have ya?" The renegade grinned.

"Some. Enough to square my bill."

"Where'd ya git hurt, and who done it?"

"Does a man have to answer them sorta questions in Lost Valley?"

"Oho, so that's the way the wind blows. How much dough ya got?"

Bart reached into the pocket of his overalls and pulled out some bank notes. The pale-eyed renegade counted them, grinned crookedly, and nodded.

"All right. Ya kin stay. But ya pull out when I tell ya to, er else run into some tough luck, savvy?"

"All I want is a place to lay down. I've had my grub."

"Ya kin sleep out amongst the trees," said the man, pocketing Bart's money. "Where's your guns?"

Bart grinned and lifted his hands. He wore no gun belt. "I'd pay you for a gun and some ca'tridges," he said.

"Got any more money?" asked the renegade shrewdly.

"Nope. But there was about a hundred there that I gave you. That orter pay for supper and a gun and a few shells, so I figgered."

"I never got no hundred. Ya trot out into the brush an' bed down. Mebbeso, if ya mind your own business and say nothin' about money to the other boys, I'll stake ya to a gun, come mornin'. But if ya make any funny kind uh play tonight, ya'll die uh lead poisonin'. Git out."

Outside, as Bart passed the men with their prisoner, he met their scrutiny with well-feigned carelessness. For the fraction of a second his eyes met Nan's. No recognition was in his glance. Nan had read his silent message.

"Hold on a minute," rasped the half-breed. "Where you goin'?"

"I'm goin' to the brush to bed," said

Bart. "The boss don't like my company around the cabin."

The half-breed looked at him closely. "I seen you somewhere before."

"Mebbeso." Bart grinned widely. "I've bin to a few places."

That seemed to tickle the Negro. "Them jails is great meetin' houses. Shucks, Pelón, you-all always a-lookin' fer trouble. This heah boy bin shot at an' hit. Ain't 'at right, Dummy?"

The other member of the sinister-looking quartet showed a toothless grin. As he opened his mouth in a soundless laugh, Bart saw that the man had no tongue. His face, lined and twisted, was the face of a man who has been into hell and has come back. Somewhere, sometime, someone had cut out the man's tongue. His soundless laugh made Bart shudder. Nan paled and turned her head aside. The ragged renegade seemed to enjoy their horror.

"Shut 'at ol' mouf, Dummy," pleaded the Negro. "It taken away ma appetite. Don' do it no mo'. Boy, git away. Git gone."

Bart limped across the clearing. He stopped where his horse was staked, and began to saddle up. The long-jawed leader of this unsavory crowd called to him.

"Where ya goin'?"

"I ain't stayin' where I ain't wanted, mister. I'll pull out."

The renegade pondered this for a long moment as he came over to Bart. His pale eyes were slitted now, deadly. The man's right hand slid along his thigh, and his hand closed over the butt of his gun.

"I reckon you're mistook. Ya ain't goin' no place. Ya seen too much fer your good health. So we'll end your misery an'. . . ."

Bart's gun slid from under the bandage. He scarcely knew that he pulled the trigger. There was that split second when he saw the man's twisted face, the bulging, horror-filled eyes. Now the boy covered the other three men. But each of them was edging toward their guns. These were not men to be bested by a wounded boy. Bart heard the rasping, horrible snarling in the throat of the renegade who lay writhing at his feet. He saw the bluish-gray look on the face of the giant Negro. He saw the tigerish eyes of the half-breed, and the gaping, toothless, tongueless mouth of the other man. They would kill him. But while they were doing it, he'd get at least one of them. Their hands were now closing over their guns. They crouched like beasts ready to spring.

Nan, her arms bound, her mouth

gagged, was forced to sit there on her horse, frozen with horror.

Then it happened. Like a bolt of lightning. Two shots that blended. Bart's gun roaring in the echo. The giant Negro went down, his eyes rolling like white marbles. The other two had been jerked upright. Their right hands both shattered, cursing, moaning.

Now a man on a black gelding was leaping from the saddle. Lee Waldron, his face a snarling mask, his two smoking guns covering the wounded men. Again Lee Waldron's quick guns had saved Bart's life.

"Take the girl away, Bart. Quick. I'm killing these filthy dogs. Get her away, boy. She mustn't see. Move, son, move!"

Never had Bart seen a man who looked as Lee Waldron now looked. His face seemed drained of blood. His lips were pulled away from his white teeth. His black eyes were like beads of red lights.

Bart's knife freed Nan of her bonds and the gag tied across her mouth. She stood there, looking at Lee Waldron, stark terror in her eyes. When she spoke, her voice was a husky whisper.

"Don't kill them," she pleaded. "Don't commit murder! They can't fight back!"

"Take her away, Bart. I'll attend to these

jackals. They're better off dead."

"Then let the law, not you, do the job!" she cried. "You're too brave a man for such a cowardly job!"

Lee Waldron bowed a little mockingly, his white teeth smiling. Then he turned to the three renegades. The man who carried Bart's bullet in his groin eyed Lee Waldron with slitted, hate-filled eyes. It was to him the killer spoke.

"Take your three foul-odored companions and get into that cabin. Stay there till the law comes to get you. Don't try to get away because the word goes out tonight to kill you-all on sight. I have men here in the hills that will gladly do the job."

The big Negro had been shot through the thigh and left a bloody trail to the cabin. The man with the lean, lantern jaw walked haltingly, his reddening hands pressed against his wound. The tongueless man and the yellow-eyed half-breed followed suit. A craven, sinister quartet that eyed Lee Waldron with fear and hatred.

The killer turned to Nan and Bart.

"I'm afraid you'll be forced to share my camp tonight. It's too far back to the ranch. I'm sorry, Miss Plunkett, that you'll have to tolerate my unwelcome company."

"Under the circumstances," said Nan with a wan smile, "I think you are most generous to include me in the invitation. I thank you."

XV

"Father and Son"

It was well past dark when they reached Lee Waldron's cabin. A small log cabin with a stone fireplace. A couple of Navajo rugs on the pine-board floor. A neat bunk built in one corner. A table, shelves filled with books, homemade chairs. Bright curtains on the windows. Their host lighted the lamp and built a fire. He made Bart lie down. He motioned to a cupboard.

"I have bandages and all else you'll need there, Miss Plunkett. Bart looks pretty much all in, and no wonder. Let's try a nip of this brandy. That'll put the blushes back in his cheeks. I'll take care of the horses and rustle supper. And since fate has thrown us together for the time being, we'll forget whatever quarrels we may have and try to enjoy the fire."

Lee Waldron proved himself a good host. He talked of everything under the skies but killing. Bart and Nan found themselves listening raptly. They forgot that he was the most dangerous man along the outlaw trail, a man hated by all men. They heard him tell of strange places in foreign countries, of music, of people, of many things.

The supper was excellent, considering the limited supply of stores. He had brought out marmalade and relishes, preserved fruit in glass jars. The meat was broiled wild turkey. His smile had lost its bitterness and his black eyes no longer looked hard. Sometimes Bart caught the man looking at him with strange intentness.

"I will be sorry to have you go tomorrow," he told them. "This is the first time I have ever had anyone stop here. Luck deals very kindly this night to a man who is undeserving of such a good break. If I begin to seem tiresome, lay it to the fact that it has been many years since I have so talked to anyone. It has been many years since man, woman, or child shared my home. Though I cannot call this a home. Not . . . not in the real sense of the word. This is just the den where the wolf hides out. I'm seldom here."

"I'd be afraid someone would steal everything while you are gone."

Lee Waldron's smile lost its pleasantness. His eyes hardened.

"Men are still paying the penalty for destroying the only real home I had. No man, good or bad, ever lifts my door latch. They are not welcome here. This is the first time anyone but Lee Waldron has ever crossed its threshold. I'm wondering if there is not something prophetic about it." And suddenly his smile was again genuine, his eyes no longer hard as he looked from the boy to the girl.

"You both have made me very happy tonight by sharing my cabin. Happier than I ever thought I would be. I am old enough to be your father. And even a man who lives like a lone wolf sometimes gets hungry for companionship."

Bart felt sorry for the man. Nan no longer looked at the killer with anger. Rather, the girl seemed to be studying him. Now she spoke.

"If our being here has made you happy, then let me say that you have made us very happy. You could make me a great deal happier if you could truthfully tell me that you will not follow my brother and shoot him down."

"I would be glad of that chance."

"If you do it, I would be forever in your debt."

"That promise was granted you before you asked it. My gun will never kill Hank Plunkett."

He rose and crossed the room toward her, his hand held out. His eyes looked down at her gravely and his smile was soft. Nan took his hand in both hers. Tears welled to her eyes. She knew that Lee Waldron was not lying.

"The law does not want Hank Plunkett or Uncle Jim Taylor. A very grave mistake has been made. I have cleared them of all charges."

"You? You cleared my brother and Uncle Jim? Why?"

"Because that is part of my job. The bounty hunter wants only hides of value."

"You say that bitterly."

"Why not? Men spit my name from their mouths when they speak of me. Yet no man can say that Lee Waldron's gun ever killed a man who did not deserve killing. Nor can any man truthfully say that the rewards I have collected were used for my own selfish purpose. Every cent I have collected has gone toward the support of widows and children whose men had been killed by some of the wolf pack that trails the hills, the human wolves that need exterminating. Only one man knows where my money goes. That man is Mike Driscoll. He only knows why Lee Waldron rides alone along the outlaw trail from Mexico to Canada, killing men or turning them in to the law. He knows why I changed my name from something else to Lee Waldron and swore to kill every man of a certain pack of outlaws that followed the outlaw trail. He knows why I turned bounty hunter. And Bart, boy, when word comes to you that Lee Waldron is dead, go to Mike Driscoll. He will tell you many things. Always remember that."

Lee Waldron now paced the cabin with that panther-like step. He halted beside the bunk, looking down at the wounded youth.

"You're a brave boy, Bart. A gentleman of courage. Is he not, Nan Plunkett?"

"He is, indeed. I know he is."

Bart reddened as Nan took his hand and held it tightly. The man smiled down at them, and Nan's cheeks flushed but she still clung to Bart's hand.

"Bart needs someone like you, Nan, to help him find many of the finer things in life. He's had it mighty tough so far. You and your brother must see that he gets those things. Books, travel, things that are his birthright. You two youngsters have found something in life without knowing that you have made the discovery. Blind little explorers. You have found that which I found once, many years ago. Men call it love. Cherish that love that is now coming into the hearts of you both. Hold to it tightly. Fight for it, worship it, honor it because it is a God-given thing.

"God once gave it to me, my children. And then, when we were the happiest people on earth, that love, that home, everything that we had prayed for together were taken from me. Taken from me by a man who owed his very life to me. A man who I had sheltered under my roof, whose wounds I had healed, whose freedom I had protected with the only lies I had ever told.

"Where our home was, does not matter here. But we had everything to make us happy. Our ranch was in the valley between high mountains. Even the wild animals lost their timidity and fear and became pets. The girl who had become my wife fed them all. It was like a little paradise on earth. Our doors were never locked. Friend or stranger found welcome there. Even the nameless men who hid from the law were welcome to food and shelter.

"Then came that bright, sunlit day in June when I left the roundup camp and rode along the trail to my ranch. I found only the smoking ashes of what had been our home. In those ashes I found the charred body of that girl who had been my wife. They had ridden away too soon to destroy all evidence. Their job had been incomplete. For her remains showed that she had been beaten to death in a brutal manner. Of our three-year-old baby there was no sign.

"When I had buried her, I took the trail. It was the trail of the man I had trusted and the human wolves who followed him. He was, so I soon came to learn, a power among those hunted men who knew no other law. His friends covered his trail, blocking me. I appealed to the state law, to the government law to aid me. We went in with a posse but could not get near them. After losing a few men, we turned back. The sheriffs told me that it was impossible to get at the men I wanted.

"So I took to the outlaw trail. Others along the lawless path were men who offered to help me. I rode with them, was one of them, and rode from Calgary to Sonora with them. Now and then fate led me to someone of that crowd that had killed my wife and baby and burned my home. When I found one of the men, I killed him. I took his carcass into town and collected what bounty the law offered. Then I would go back. The trail led to Mexico, to South America, to Alaska, and even to Europe. I trailed them down, one at a time. One by one I killed them. I collected the bounty offered for them and gave it all to the one man in the world who I could trust. Mike Driscoll. For it was Shannon Driscoll who had been my bride. Shannon Driscoll, Mike Driscoll's only daughter.

"And so, for sixteen years, I followed the outlaw trail. I killed men. I made them fear my name. Not my real name, but the name of Lee Waldron. Sometimes I changed it. But always I came back to it when I hunted one of that jackal pack. So they would know who trailed them.

"The fools kept adding to the reward on my head. They keep the reward money posted in cash at Mike Driscoll's. They don't know that Mike Driscoll hates 'em like he hates snakes.

"Bill Bolin was one of 'em. Bart, you saw his finish. There are a few more. That tongueless brute and the one with the long jaw are two more. There are others yet to wipe out.

"Nan, I hunted Hank Plunkett because

they told me he was one of the crowd. Somebody lied. Bill Bolin, I think. This devil who is the real man I want has ways of working that are proof of the fact that he is a genius at crime and trickery.

"I think that I have him spotted. If my plan works out, he will walk into my trap. When he does, he dies. And when he is dead, my job is done. I can then push back my chair and quit the game. . . ."

Bart and Nan, still holding tightly to each other's hand, had listened in silence to the story Lee Waldron told. The man looked older, somehow. Sadness, rather than bitter cruelty, lined his handsome face. He stood there, hands on his guns, staring into the open fire, the shadows playing across his dark eyes.

Nan reached out and took his hand. Her eyes were misted, her voice low and soft.

"Won't you please tell us, please, about . . . her? About Shannon Driscoll?"

Lee Waldron smiled at them. He nodded and released his hand. From his pocket he took a leather-bound case. Without a word he handed it to the girl.

Reverently, gently, Nan opened the leather case. Inside were three photographs. One of a man in his early twenties. One of a girl with the face of a Madonna.

One of a small boy in an old-fashioned little suit.

For a moment Nan stared at the pictures. Her face seemed to turn a little pale and her lips parted in a soundless question. She looked at Bart, then at Lee Waldron. The man nodded, his smile wistful, a little questioning. His hands no longer were on his guns, but were gripped together behind his back.

"Then Bart is . . . ?"

"Is my son. My boy . . . and hers. And may heaven and Shannon and her baby son have mercy on me."

Lee Waldron met Bart's eyes. Bart's one good arm went out and across the shoulders of the man who had dropped on his knees beside the bunk.

The cracking of the log fire was the only sound that broke the silence of the cabin. Nan's eyes were wet with tears. Father and son were too overcome by emotion to speak.

Now, from outside, the nicker of a horse. Lee Waldron tensed. On his feet now, he crossed to the table and extinguished the lamp. He slid heavy shutters across the windows and barred the door.

"Perhaps," said Nan, "it is one of your men coming."

The firelight threw shadows across the killer's handsome face.

"I was just bluffing those renegades. I have no men. Lee Waldron fights alone."

"Not any more," said Bart.

Dirt from a box was thrown on the fire. The cabin was now in utter darkness. Nan was close to Bart, the perfume of her hair in his nostrils. Her lips brushed his cheek. Then Bart's arm was around her and their lips met in the darkness. So they pledged their betrothal.

Then Bart crouched beside his father, a gun in his hand. From out yonder in the darkness came the creaking of saddle leather, the rattle of spurs, the pounding of hoofs. Voices. Voices of the renegade pack who hated and feared Lee Waldron. The pack of human wolves that were closing in for their kill. Creeping, crouching black shadows that moved among the pines like evil things.

XVI

"End of the Trail"

There was a trap door that led to a small cellar where Lee Waldron kept his supplies. Against Nan's protests that she wanted to stay beside Bart, the men made her climb down into the dark space, out of line of any bullets.

The men outside opened fire with a vicious volley that rattled like hail against the door and heavy shutters. A few of the bullets droned through the door and thudded into the log wall above the bunk.

Bart and Lee Waldron returned the fire. Lee Waldron's rifle was taking toll, judging from the yelps of pain out yonder in the black shadows.

"Just a pack of yellow-backed coyotes, Bart. They're afraid to rush us. Afraid to die." He laughed a little.

The cabin was built for just such an emergency. Loopholes through which they poked their gun barrels, the thick door and shutters, the cabin itself in the middle of the clearing so that any men attacking would make excellent targets. An abundance of food, several canteens filled with water besides the filled pail. Plenty of ammunition. They could stand a long siege here in the stout cabin.

Above the other sounds, when the firing lessened, could be heard the hoarse, snarling voice of a man. At the sound of that voice Bart gave a sudden start.

"Gosh!" he said. "I'd know that voice in a million. That's old Haddock out there!"

"Quite so, Bart. The old rascal has been here in the rough hills for almost a week. He came after you himself when the law failed in their effort to take you back to Montana. You're worth money to him, son. In fact, it's you, not Haddock, as he now calls himself, who really owns the Figure 8 outfit."

"Me?"

"You, Bart. Haddock was the man that killed your mother and stole you. He used another name then, but it's the same man. Why he stole you, I don't know. But steal you he did and gave you into the care of some people in Wyoming. They got right fond of you, this man and wife who ran a roadhouse and way station for outlaws. The man made a will leaving you all he had in case his wife died. Smallpox took both of 'em and you were left a nice little fortune. But Haddock got himself appointed your guardian, juggled some papers around through a crooked lawyer, thus giving him full control of the money. He slipped into Montana and used that money to buy the Figure 8 Ranch. He was appointed manager of the ranch. In case you died, the ranch would go to him. He did his best to starve you to death. He planned on your death before you reached the age of twenty-one and learned the fact that you, not Haddock, owned the outfit. He'd like to get you back to murder you. But he wants the murder to look as if it was an accident of some kind. Or sickness.

"For sixteen years I've tried to locate that man. But a bad accident had crippled him and changed his appearance. He used another name than the one he'd used when I knew him. I'd hunted all over half the world hoping to find him. It was Mike Driscoll who, when he saw you, began to sniff along a new trail. When you got hurt, we laid the trap for Haddock. Knew he'd come here to get you . . . I'd planned on getting him. Then you youngsters quarreled and both rode up here. And here we are. Haddock's man trailed you. It was not my trail Nan followed. So here we three are with that murdering snake and his renegades playing us a tune or two on their rifles. . . . But Haddock will never get you, Son. Nor will any one of those brutes lay a hand on Nan or you. We'll hold 'em off until help comes. Then this man who calls himself Haddock will find himself caught in his own trap."

"You think help is coming?" asked Bart.

"I reckon so, Son. Mike Driscoll has been keeping an eye on Haddock and his dirty crew. Mike will be showing up after a bit, I hope. Till he gets here, it's up to you and me, Bart. With Mike will be the best and gamest peace officer in the country, Pat Bartlett. Pat is the man who rode twenty miles through as bad a blizzard as ever hit Colorado to bring the doctor the night you were born. Pat Bartlett was then my wagon boss. You were named after him, boy. Your real name is Bartlett Lee."

A shadow moved out yonder and Lee Waldron's gun cracked. A brief laugh came from the killer as a voice out there in the black shadows yelped like a whipped cur.

"He got that slug in the leg, Bart. Just where I wanted it put. I'm shooting low tonight. Could have killed him, but I'm done with killing. There is only one man on earth that I hope to kill. That man is the one who killed your mother. Then my game here is done."

Now Lee Waldron raised his voice so that it carried to Nan who crouched in the little cellar.

"How are you getting along there, Nan?"

"Great, thanks."

"Stout little liar, Nan. Game girl."

"If you'd let me up out of this place and give me my Twenty-Five-Twenty," she complained, "I'd feel more human. I bet there's mice in this cellar."

"She'd kill a man but would run from a mouse." Lee Waldron chuckled.

The cabin was filled with powder smoke by now, and the crack of the guns was deafening. The darkness inside was opaque. Outside was the white light of a quarter moon. Bart and Lee Waldron stood at opposite sides of the cabin, thus commanding a view on these two sides. Waldron made Bart take a stiff drink of brandy now and then, for he knew that the boy's shoulder must be giving him pain.

It seemed like some strange dream to Bart that he should be here with his own father and with the girl he loved, fighting against old Haddock and Haddock's tough cowboys. Now he remembered that half-breed who had been with the Negro and the other two renegades. That half-breed had worked for Haddock, had gotten into a killing scrape up there, and had to quit the country.

The firing increased. Someone using steel-jacket bullets was ripping shot after shot through the door. The heavy-calibered slugs smashed into the logs. Bart reckoned that was Haddock's shooting. The old rascal was a crack shot and used a heavy-calibered gun.

"If only he'd show himself," gritted Lee Waldron. But Haddock had no intention of showing himself.

Once, under the cursing tongue of Haddock, the renegades tried to rush the cabin. Bart and Lee Waldron sent them back to cover quickly.

Now, from beyond, came the roaring battle cry of big Mike Driscoll. His bellowing voice filled the night. Behind its echoes came the shrill yells of the cowboy posse with him. One voice yelped with wild abandon.

"Hank!" cried Nan. "That's Hank's yell!"

Now the renegades broke and ran for their horses. Lee Waldron jerked open the door, calling to Bart to close it after him.

Bart saw the killer running for the timber. Saw a crimson flame break from the pines as some hidden man shot at him. Lee Waldron stumbled, caught himself, kept on running, dodging as he ran, a six-shooter in each hand. Now those two guns began belching flame. The hidden man was returning the fire. Bart saw the man who was his father standing in a patch of moonlight swaying a little, his two guns spewing fire until the guns were empty. Then the man turned and walked back to the cabin.

Mike Driscoll, Sheriff Pat Bartlett, Hank Plunkett, and Jim Taylor came riding across the clearing now. Just as Lee Waldron reached the cabin, Bart flung open the door. Across Lee Waldron's gray flannel shirt front was a widening crimson stain. His face looked pale. He smiled and held out the two empty guns to Bart.

"They're yours, Son. I won't ever need 'em again. They're empty. Never load them again, Bart. You'll find twelve bullets in the man you call Haddock. Good bye Son. I'm at the end of the trail."

Bart caught the reeling form in his arms. The two beautiful guns slid to the ground. Lee Waldron was dead.

Lee Waldron, killer, had come to the end of the trail. And where his trail ended there began the trail of Bartlett Lee, cowboy.

Uncle Jim Taylor preached the funeral sermon the next morning.

"I am the resurrection and the life . . . he that. . . ."

And when Lee Waldron had been buried there among the tall pines, after Mike Driscoll and Hank and Uncle Jim and the tall sheriff had paid their last respects to the dead man, they rode away. Only Bart and Nan stood there by the little cabin.

Then, after a time, they got their horses and rode along the trail. They found the grulla mule tied to a tree beside the trail. Pinned to the pack was a note:

Foller this grulla mule. He's wiser than a heap of men. He'll lead you to the nearest preacher, then down along the trail to a ranch where he'll stop and no human bein' kin make him move on further. Fetch the preacher with you. Us boys will be waitin' there to give you two a fittin' and proper fiesta. I got a marker in the Book where the weddin' services is kep', so tell the sky pilot he needn't lug his Book along. Just foller that grulla mule. See you later.

Uncle Jim

About the Author

Walt Coburn was born in White Sulphur Springs, Montana Territory. He was once called "King of the Pulps" by Fred Gipson and promoted by Fiction House as "The Cowboy Author." He was the son of cattleman, Robert Coburn, then owner of the Circle C ranch on Beaver Creek within sight of the Little Rockies. Coburn's family eventually moved to San Diego while still operating the Circle C. Robert Coburn used to commute between Montana and California by train, and he would take his youngest son with him. When Coburn got drunk one night, he had an argument with his father that led to his leaving the family. In the course of his wanderings he entered Mexico and for a brief period actually became an enlisted man in the so-called *gringo* battalion of Pancho Villa's army.

Following his enlistment in the U.S.

Army during the Great War, Coburn began writing Western short stories. For a year and a half he wrote and wrote before selling his first story to Bob Davis, editor of *Argosy All-Story*. Coburn married and moved to Tucson because his wife suffered from a respiratory condition. In a little adobe hut behind the main house Coburn practiced his art and for almost four decades he wrote approximately 600,000 words a year. Coburn's early fiction from his Golden Age — 1924–1940 — is his best, including his novels, *Mavericks* (1929) and *Barb Wire* (1931), as well as many short novels published only in magazines that now are being collected for the first time. In his Western stories, as Charles M. Russell and Eugene Manlove Rhodes, two men Coburn had known and admired in life, he captured the cow country and recreated it just as it was already passing from sight. *South of the Law Line* will be his next Five Star Western.

The employees of Thorndike Press hope you have enjoyed this Large Print book. All our Thorndike and Wheeler Large Print titles are designed for easy reading, and all our books are made to last. Other Thorndike Press Large Print books are available at your library, through selected bookstores, or directly from us.

For information about titles, please call:

(800) 223-1244

or visit our Web site at:

www.gale.com/thorndike
www.gale.com/wheeler

To share your comments, please write:

Publisher
Thorndike Press
295 Kennedy Memorial Drive
Waterville, ME   04901